THE BOYFRIEND BOOK

THE BOYFRIEND BOOK

Written by: Michael E. Reid

Dreams On Paper Entertainment Publishing

PHILADELPHIA

Also by Michael E. Reid

Dear Woman
Just Words
Just Words 2

Cover Design: Roberto Núñez
Layout & Design: Jermaine Lau and Roberto Nunez

For permission requests, please contact the publisher at:

Mango Publishing Group
2850 Douglas Road, 2nd Floor
Coral Gables, FL 33134 USA
info@mango.bz

For special orders, quantity sales, course adoptions
and corporate sales, please email the publisher at
sales@mango.bz. For trade and wholesale sales, please
contact Ingram Publisher Services at customer.service@
ingramcontent.com or +1.800.509.4887.

Library of Congress Cataloging
ISBN: (print) 978-1-63353-846-7 (ebook) 978-1-63353-847-4
Library of Congress Control Number: 2018962511
BISAC category code: POE023020—POETRY / Subjects & Themes
/ Love & Erotica

Printed in the United States of America

The Boyfriend Book

Written for: _____

Gifted by: _____

I will not stop.
Until every woman finds her crown.
Because not enough men see the value in something,
unless it's shining.
So now we've got to blind them...

Table of Contents

Yesterday 16

If You Have a Woman 25

Around Their Hearts 29

The Promise 32

Prayer 37

Beast 42

What If 47

You Must Be Ready 54

When They Ask Me Why I'm Single 57

Shelter 67

Him 74

Time 81

Whatever You Do 87

Safe 93

Power 101

Layaway 109

Bird 118

Exit 123

No Boyfriend, No Problem 128

Heal 133

Selma 136

Reciprocity 141

Reservations 146

Crazy 154

Mirror 162

Groundhog Day 165

Enough 168

When It's Real 171

Together 173

Crown 176

Extra 179

When He Left 182

I'm in Your Corner 186

If 189

Running 192

I'm Ready for Love 196

When Men Get Married 201

To the Women

When you read this book, I want you to know that this world is a dangerous place on its own, and it is even more dangerous when you have to let strangers in. I wrote this book as a precautionary measure. For some women, it could be just a different way of looking at a particular subject, but for other women, this book could be a way for you to change your life. The possibilities are endless, but are also, ultimately, up to you. The only thing that I can say is this: I need you to ask yourself where you were before you opened this book. Then I need you to figure out where you want to be. Then see how this book can be used to get you there.

In a perfect world, I would want to believe that you can meet somebody and commit to them and not have to worry about anything else, because everybody in the world would be good, and everybody in the world would have your best interests at heart. But everybody knows that everybody in the world isn't like that.

Unfortunately, while some women are pretty decent judges of character, some women don't see the train coming until it hits them.

I wrote this book for you, specifically you, about this one specific topic. I just hope you appreciate it and enjoy it as much as I did.

Read it slow. Plant the seed. Let it grow.

Sincerely,

Michael E. Reid

YESTERDAY

I met a woman
On a bridge.
On a ledge.
On the edge.
Of love and light.
Of day and night.
Of life.
And I asked her for advice.
And she said:
Some will hurt you a lot.
Some will hurt you a little.
Some will hurt you on the outside.
Some will hurt you in the middle.
But you will heal.
Some will waste your money.
Others, your time.
The worst: both.
But at the end of the rope,
there's hope.
So, you'll be fine.
You must.
Or you'll bust.
And from the tears in her eyes,
I knew.
She was finished.
She jumped.
Died falling.
Died from falling.
The irony is appalling.
A life story that could never
be worth applauding.

Or could it?
Maybe, if I told her story.
Gave her death some glory.
Then maybe God will see her
as a martyr and have mercy.
She'll show up at the gates, soaking wet.
Covered in water and regret.
And when he asks her why she jumped,
She'll tell him she was thirsty.
And they will laugh.
And he will forgive her for her sin.
And let her in.
Because her only flaw was loving hard.
Wanted rock. Wound up sinking.
No preserver.
Death certificate says suicide.
I call it
murder.
And he'll get away with it.
But this isn't a reality show.
Because sometimes
When you're in love,
The reality goes.
And you're standing there.
In a bunch of feelings you didn't even
know you had,
And part of you
is going to want to yell, "Dad."
But you can't because you're grown.
And you should never
have brought him home
In the first place.
I know it hurts,
But it's taking longer to heal

than it should have.
Think about the kind of man you could have.
If it was supposed to work, it would have.
Disappointment is certain.
Healing is on purpose.
So, before you fall into the darkness,
Pull back the curtains.
You must make the rest of your life
The best of your life
If you hope to have any life at all.
So, remember this woman
the next time you fall.
Yesterday, I met a woman
On a bridge.
On a ledge.
On the edge.
Of love and light.
Of day and night.
Of life.
And she asked me for advice.
And I told her,
Heavy is the head of a woman who carries her crown.
And when love leaves you in unfamiliar territory,
It is much easier to drown.
But the same courage that you used to fall in love,
You must find after.
I'm no preacher or pastor,
But I do know
that only God can put a smile where a frown was.
So, if you still do decide to jump,
I pray that God catches you
Before the ground does.

This year, an estimated one hundred thousand women will contemplate suicide because of a "boyfriend." Seven thousand will be successful. One is too many.

National Suicide Prevention Lifeline

1-800-273-8255

To the Good Men

First and foremost, I'm not the enemy. I know a lot of what I write seems a little bit "one-sided," and it also may seem a little bit woman-centered, but I do it because I think that women are probably the most underappreciated asset on earth. I apologize if you feel like I haven't fed you enough. I know that I haven't, and I don't anticipate things being like this forever. But what you have to understand is that there are some women in some serious danger. And some of them don't even know it. When I first started this journey, there weren't too many people out here to help them. I come from a history of personally helping women starting with my mother, and then it just ballooned to the world. And now, after seeing its success, I have to take flight with it. I want you to know that I think about you with every word that I write. I am one of you. While I don't always write to you, I most certainly write for you.

To the Others

I feel like through no fault of our own as individual men, the playing field has become too one-sided in our favor. So as a man, I have two options. I can either accept that, or I can do something to possibly level the playing field. I have chosen option B: to make it my purpose to be a vessel to save women. Sometimes it's to save them from themselves; sometimes it's to save them from some of us.

Unfortunately, to some men, that has come across as me "not giving good men credit" or me "uplifting women at the expense of men." If you feel that way, then I apologize. But at the end of the day, I don't think I've ever said anything that specifically targeted men as a whole. I feel like I do target a certain type of man, though, I'll admit that. I am hard on the type of man who doesn't necessarily value women as much as I do, which in turn makes them feel a certain kind of way. To them, the ones who take issue with what I do simply because it raises a woman's bar to some new height, women who may subsequently remove these men from their lives? To those men, my response is, "Sorry. Not sorry."

Nothing makes me happier as an artist and as a man than seeing the looks on women's faces when they read my poems, when they read my posts, and when they tell me that what I wrote was the reason they "got better."

It makes them happy, it makes me happy, and we're not bothering you.

To the World

I know what it feels like to be alone. I also know what it feels like to be with someone and still feel like you're alone. Only one of those "alones" makes you strong. This is especially true when that "somebody" was the person you thought you didn't have to worry about–the person you thought you were safe with, only for them to turn out to be the person you worry about the most.

I know what it's like to put everything you have into one person and then for them to wake up one day and tell you that they don't want you anymore–even when you didn't do anything but be you the entire time. I know what it feels like for somebody to tell you that "you" wasn't enough.

I know what it feels like to be scared about your future, about your happiness, because your whole life you thought happiness meant one thing, but more importantly, you thought you had to go to one place to get it. So, before we continue, I want you to know it gets better. I am proof that it gets better.

Lastly, I want you to think about what love is. I want you to think about what happiness is. And I want you to ask yourself, at its core, at its bare minimum, how many people does it take for you to have it, to have both love and happiness? Hopefully the answer is "one" and that one person is you. But if for some reason that's not your answer, and you feel like you have to be with somebody else to make you feel good, to make you feel loved, or to make you feel happy, then I want you to put as much effort into finding that person as you do into making it work with that person.

Welcome to *The Boyfriend Book*.

To the Couples

I am a fan of love more than anything else. Couples are the reason why I may not have wanted to write this book before, because the last thing most relationships want is to have people from the outside attempting to affect what's happening on the inside. But I can't deny what's on my heart. I can't tell myself that I'll feel okay if I don't let people know how I feel about a certain subject, and right now, that subject just happens to be boyfriends.

What I don't want this book to do is make two people question a bond that didn't otherwise have any issues before somebody decided to read it. I don't want this book to break up happy homes, because it takes so much to make a home, and the people in it, happy. So hopefully, my book will make strong bonds stronger, not weaker.

To the other couples, the ones who might be struggling, but are sticking around because of comfort or convenience? To those people, I say, please read this book carefully. Read to understand, not just to comprehend.

Sometimes people are put in your life for certain reasons, but not the reasons you thought. Maybe this book will help you sort out some things with some people. If that sorting leads to separation, then I pray that you find peace on the other side.

IF YOU HAVE A WOMAN

Who's strong enough to be alone,
But soft enough to still allow
a place in her heart for you,
Take her by the hand.
And if you're not man enough
To lead her through the darkness yet,
At least be brave enough
to not let her stand in it alone.
Appreciate her flaws.
Because, sometimes, the same reasons
why the world tells her
She's not good enough…
Are the same reasons she may appreciate you
For loving her anyway.
If you have a woman
Who's woman enough to lie in an empty bed
for the rest of her life
Because she refuses to lie
next to a man who loves her body
More than her mind,
And she gives you the pleasure of having her
however you please:
Make love to her like the world is on fire.
Like every argument you ever had
will be forgotten.
Like the cure for her insecurities
Is your fingertips
Playing piano with the parts of her body
That she has yet to fall in love with
To the point where the gates
of her own personal heaven

Have no choice but to pour
onto the bedroom comforter.
Comfort her with your presence.
Drown yourself in her sea of serenity.
Because the more often she comes,
The less likely she'll go elsewhere.
The only thing worse than a woman
Who is too scared to love
Is the man
Who is too scared to love her back.

June 1, 2016

This book was the hardest one yet to write, hard because I finally had to sit down and think about one subject. I pride myself in having a lot to say. I pride myself even more on my diversity and freedom. So when you put me in a box, when I put me in a box, my first reaction is to escape. Unfortunately, sometimes when you're running, it isn't always a good thing. Sometimes you can be running from yourself, from your purpose, from what you were put here to do.

And for the last year, that's what I've been doing.

There has been a lot of pressure on me since *Dear Woman*, and most of it has been self-inflicted. I never expected that book to sell as much as it did, to reach as many people as it did, or to be as influential as it was to women. I wrote that book in eighteen hours, three days before it was released. All I had was a notepad full of topics, my heart, and God. It subsequently singlehandedly changed my life. It put me in a place where I realized that my purpose was to be a voice to speak to women— of honesty, encouragement, support, and hope. In the process, I realized that my work has truly only just begun. *Dear Woman* did a lot of good for both me and the world. It gave me freedom; it gave the people who read it validation, insight, and a little humor. Another thing I realized it did was that it raised some women's bar. It changed what they stood for, who they stood for. It let them know that they weren't crazy. It also let them know that they might need to evaluate some of the relationships they were in. What it didn't do enough of was tell enough people how to do that.

AROUND THEIR HEARTS

Made with bricks from other men.
And I see men like me
on the other side of these walls.
Trying to get in.
And the only thing that's stopping us is them.
Is him.
And he isn't even here.
But he left you this wall,
So guys like me can't make it over to catch the tears.
Because they still fall.
Because it's been over a year
and he still hasn't called.
And you don't know if you miss love, or him.
All you'll know is that right now,
you could use a friend.
But the same wall that protects you from him
Keeps me out too.
Meanwhile you're on the other side.
And you can't remember
that last time that you made love,
Or cried.
All you know is that this wall
is what protects you from the demons.
From the liars
Who take a perfectly good woman
and set her soul on fire,
Then leave for no reason.
A woman with a wall up must learn amnesia,
Or buy a ladder
If she ever hopes to be rescued.
Because no matter how much he could love you,

He can never let you.
So, the next time you look at your wall,
See what it's made of.
You'll realize that the whole thing was made up.

A woman
Is only going to be as strong
As the things
She gets through.
If at every opportunity
That life gives you
To let something go,
You choose
To hold on tighter,
The only thing
You're really hurting
Is yourself.

THE PROMISE

Let what we build here
Stand the tests of time,
The tests of this crazy world,
And the tests of love.
In your darkest of moments,
When you can't seem to find
the shade of makeup
to magnify your melanin,
When the only thing more confusing
than your past
is your future
And the presents
aren't coming in fast enough...
I pray that you will always find your way to
either the mall
Or my arms.
Because anything your money can't buy
A good man will make you feel
like you don't even need.
Together we will conquer
anything life throws at us.
Use me.
To heal whichever part of your soul hurts.
To fill whatever voids some man left
the day he realized you were
Too much woman.
Find Me.
Or find enough peace, patience, and power
to reject the things
you cannot change.
Enough gas left in the tank

to drive toward the things you can,
And enough sober nights to know the difference.
When you're at a fork in the road
Between the woman you are,
and the woman someone else wants you to be,
Adjust your crown.
Remember how long it took for you to get here,
How hard you fought to become her.
Promise that who you are,
who you want to be,
and whom you decide to love
Will always be your choice,
On your terms,
And never, ever, conflict
with what you stand for.

Change

So when I finally decided on what my next book would be, I was hyped. Just like some of the women, I didn't know where to go after *Dear Woman*. Then I came up with *The Boyfriend Book*. The concept? I felt like *Dear Woman* left a lot of women single. So, I was going to write a book to "keep them occupied."

I came up with the title when I did an interview for a blogger from London. She asked me, if had one wish, what would it be? The first thing that came to mind was, I would wish to meet my wife tomorrow. She thought it was the sweetest thing ever. We went on to talk about why I wanted love so bad, and if I ever thought I would find it. So after I hung up the phone, I sat and I thought, "That's pretty selfish, to have one wish that you know is going to come true, and you use it to only help you." So I thought about it some more, and I came up with, "Being every woman's first boyfriend." I called the blogger back and told her I wanted to change my answer. At first, she thought I was crazy, but when I broke it down to her, she started crying. That's when I knew I was onto something…

I told her, "I want to be every woman's first boyfriend because I want to set the table, set the bar, set the precedent for what you believe in, for what you call love. That way, at least when we break up, as you will eventually do with every boyfriend who doesn't become your husband, at least the next person will be a good person."

You know that's how it's supposed to work, right? Make a list of all the "boyfriends" you've had, from the first one till now. Do the relationships get better as you get older? If not, then maybe the problem isn't in who's chosen, but in the chooser. So, I had a plan. My next book was going to be me writing a year's worth of love letters to women. I was going to be their "boyfriend." Imagine coming home to a book that you could read that was filled with love—filled with hope.

It was beautiful—until my ninety-eight-year-old grandmother, who is still by the grace of God very much alive and well, asked me what my new book was going to be about. And when I told her what I just told you, her response was, "That's stupid."

PRAYER

Would you mind it if I prayed for you?
Dear God,
Let this woman.
The one you made from my rib.
The one who made you take the next day off
so you could worship what you just did.
May the first man she raises be her kid.
And not one of these boys
…who use their toys to distract her
from doing her homework.
…who would only consider giving her the world
if she promises to take them home first.
I pray that you always remember that you're the catch.
That the battle is for your mind and the reward is the sex.
That when they become bad for you,
You become good at ignoring their texts.
May the space between where she is
and where she wants to be
Be filled with good vibes and better company.
When she's alone and in her feelings,
Wondering why she isn't already
married with children,
Give her patience.
Let her hold out for a man that's better than basic.
One safe enough for her to tell her wildest dreams,
And crazy enough to help her chase them.
May he be so close that she can taste it.
And if he's not,
Give her enough confidence to call her own shots.
Enough common sense to call the cops.
Because it's a crime to be out here

getting treated less than
"Beyoncé."
May the progression of her partnership be
best friend turned fiancé.
Until then,
Bless this young queen with enough options
That she starts to feel like a priority.
And what she lacks in confidence,
let her make up for in authority.
Reach her. Teach her.
To always love the skin that she's in.
Promise to protect her from anything not sent by you
And forgive her for her sins.

Amen.

God and Love

These are two of the greatest stories ever told, though they are not often enough connected. "Boyfriend" is no exception. Maybe it's because if you loved God as much as you could, you would notice that the man you loved really wasn't a man at all, and it would force you to change. Maybe it's because you did love God, and then you met this man, and this man became more of a wedge than a bridge between you and God. Maybe you didn't know God before you knew love. And as you grew closer to God, you grew further away from your boyfriend. In any of these cases, there is a woman torn between a man and a myth. If she is not careful, if she is not strong, if she doesn't believe in something other than this man, then she will live and die by the presence of a man who has yet to promise that he will never leave her.

I cannot express enough the value, the peace, the comfort, of having a man who fears not only you, but also God. If God orders his steps and you follow this man, it's like you are going in the direction in which you were already going, but now you have company. I don't know who this book may reach. I'm not sure what God, if any, they believe in. All I can say is that there must be something other than things like physical attraction, convenience, or history to bind two people together. If not, when these things fade away, so will the love. Why? Because love is only as strong as the foundation it is built on. What better bricks with which to lay the foundation for longevity than a love that has lasted over two thousand years?

In a perfect world, life is good. You will have your man, you will have your God, and, together, the three of you will build a wall of love, hope, and respect; of trust, prayer, and faith. And as the three of you grow together, this wall will become higher—high enough that the negative won't be able to climb over and reach you.

The problem is that after the wall is built, sometimes not all of you are on the same side. So the question is, which side do you pick? You pick you. You pick possibility. You say to yourself, it's going to take all three of us. After that, the math should be easy. You will always have you. God is everywhere, so the only thing left to do is find a man who loves you both.

BEAST

To the ones who don't look like what they've been through.
The ones who have a pain in their heart
that from time to time still puts
a tear or two in their eyes...
Still, they manage
To wake up every morning with a smile on their face,
When just last year, last week, last night,
They were face to face with a demon
Disguised as a friend.
I see you.
Everyone won't know your journey.
Nor should they have to.
Just keep pushing.
Until you're pregnant with possibility,
Swollen with self-love,
Covered in confidence.
Dominate the doubters
dedicated to documenting your demise.
Be Beast.
In a world where they only want you
to be pretty and quiet,
Curse your critics with enough conviction
to counter your cadence.
And if you ever
Become more mush than mantle,
More punching bag than pile driver,
Look no further than your reflection.
A reminder that you are woman.
That you are here.
That you will not go quietly.
Make memories of your enemies.

Family of your friends.
And the rest of your life the best of your life.
All you've got is what you have.
Make it all you need.
And when the strangers approach,
If they are not safe enough to let them pet your mane,
May your roar be loud enough
to keep them at bay.

Research

When I asked my grandmother what she meant when she called my book stupid, she reminded me that she was born in 1918. She told me that when she was old enough to "date," there was no such thing as a "boyfriend." "If a man wanted you, he would marry you." Before I jumped up and tried to explain to her how things are different now, I asked myself, am I listening to understand, or am I listening just to reply—like most people do when someone is trying to sell them something other than whatever they believe in? I decided to live to fight another day, and I kindly thanked her for the conversation and went home. When I got home, I Googled everything I could about the word "boyfriend."

The more I dug into researching the word, the more my mind was blown. I was at a loss for words. Here was this word that I had used ever since I was old enough to be able to afford to take a girl to the movies (which was age thirteen, by the way). This word was the reason why I always dressed nicely, why I went out of my way to talk to every pretty girl I saw. When I was first introduced to love, it was through the idea of "boyfriend."

That idea changed when I opened the dictionary and looked it up, just like you're supposed to do with any other word that you use, especially one you use to define your happiness, to identify the role of the most important person in your life not related to you. So many people use the word "boyfriend" and don't even know what it really means. Let's test a theory.

If you're reading this, you have probably heard the word "boyfriend" before. I would push the envelope a little further and say that not only have you heard the word, you probably know what it means. So if you know what a word means, that means you know its definition. Where do we get definitions? The dictionary. Here are three sources, all of them saying pretty much the same thing; but for me, it was all about what they didn't say.

boyfriend (boi·frĕnd)
Noun
1. A male companion or friend with whom one has a sexual or romantic relationship.
2. A male friend.
Source: The American Heritage® Dictionary of the English Language, Fifth Edition, copyright ©2015 by Houghton Mifflin Harcourt Publishing Company. All rights reserved.

boy·friend \boi· frĕnd\
Simple Definition of **boyfriend**: a man that someone is having a romantic or sexual relationship with
Source: Merriam-Webster's Learner's Dictionary

boy· friend
/boi/frend
Noun
1. A regular male companion or friend with whom one has a sexual or romantic relationship.
Synonyms: lover, sweetheart, beloved, darling, dearest, man, guy, escort
Source: Google Dictionary

WHAT IF

What if I told you that "boyfriend" didn't exist?
Would you believe me?
What if I took it a step further and said that the
idea of a "boyfriend" (to include missing one, wanting one,
accepting "boyfriend" as a necessary step in the process
of you going from single to married)
would be the biggest roadblock
you could ever face?
Would you take my word for it?
What if I told you that while the idea
of having a boyfriend could possibly be one
of the most pleasurable seasons in your life,
in the long run it could ultimately
do more harm than good?
Would you erase every memory of it?
Of the word. Of the title. Of the need.
Probably not.
Don't worry. At first, I didn't either.
But I have studied. I have prayed.
And I have come to a conclusion:
If the ultimate goal for you is marriage,
There is no fundamental need for a boyfriend
to achieve it…
And I have found no concrete evidence to
contradict this theoretical goal.
So, therefore, having a boyfriend becomes an option.
Not mandatory.
I am going to use stories, poems, experiences,
Over the next hundred pages or so,
Both personal and professional,
To convince you that while I know

every woman loves options,
and some—just as many—love the idea of
coming home to someone,
Counting on someone to be there when no one else is,
Making love to someone
(Including you sometimes),
Someone to be your rock, your special place,
Or whatever emotional, spiritual,
or inspirational quote you
attach to someone you care about…
I am here to convince you, to warn you,
to set you up for success.
By saying that someone this powerful could never be just a
boyfriend.

Option vs. Obligation

For me, why somebody does something is just as important as what they do. If you agree, and if we apply this thinking to relationships, then it's my opinion that being in a relationship makes it hard for you to realize whether someone is doing something because they want to or because it's what they are supposed to do. I believe that "boyfriend" and "relationships" turn what used to be an option into an obligation. Let's start from the beginning.

courtship /kohrt·ship/ noun

Simple Definition of **courtship**

1. Somewhat old-fashioned: the activities that occur when people are developing a romantic relationship that could lead to marriage or the period of time when such activities occur

Source: Merriam-Webster's Learner's Dictionary

When you met a man, if the year was around, say, 1930 to 1940, the courting process would begin. This would carry all the way through until marriage. It was sort of like a man's audition to be your co-star. This courtship has evolved to what we now all know as dating. The problem is, the dating doesn't last as long as the courtship. The next stop isn't wife any more, it's girlfriend. This changes what a man does for you from being an option to being an obligation. This makes it more like work, and less like play. Where it messes things up is that a woman can't tell if the act is coming from the kindness of his heart or because he feels like this is what he has to do, because of his title. No boyfriend, no problem.

Why?

So the million-dollar question is, why do I want to write a book that cautions women against ever having a boyfriend? The first reason is parents. I believe it's your parents' job to protect you from the world as best they can, for as long as they can, until you're smart enough, strong enough, and equipped with enough to deal with this world on your own. Your parents are either going to be your strongest asset or your most frustrating liability, depending upon how supportive your family is or isn't. Without ignoring all of the other ways that a family can let you down, I want to focus specifically on the relationship aspect.

I wish that every parent would be as honest as possible with their children about love, and tell them not what they want their children to believe about it, but the truth. I feel like if more parents told their children the truth about love, then a lot more people would be set up for relationship success, especially women. I am not a parent. but I often ask myself what I would tell my daughter about men and about boyfriends.

Hopefully, my daughter will witness what true love looks like at first hand, in the home. She will use this as the basis for what she looks for in love. She will not need to turn to television, movies, social media, or other people, because true love does not live in a vacuum. She will need to experience firsthand the day-to-day sacrifices and arguments that love requires. Second, my daughter will understand that the love she witnesses her parents giving each other was the result of effort. She will understand how this effort was a two-part process. More importantly, she will understand that this love is the fruit of that labor.

The labor was not "making it work" with somebody, but being patient enough to wait for the person who makes it not even feel like work.

One day, my daughter is going to want to date. So, what do I tell her? Most parents are fearful of this day. Most parents aren't sure if they have equipped their daughters with the knowledge and skills needed to interact with men. So they treat the dating process like it's a phase, hoping that she will eventually find someone, so that they as parents no longer have to worry about their daughter and her safety.

Most parents don't have the courage to tell their daughter to never have a boyfriend. There's too much at risk. So, they encourage boyfriends because they see them as the lesser of two evils. Parents would rather see you with one boy than to have different ones popping up at their front door every weekend. So they encourage this pre-marriage monogamy because it puts their hearts at ease. This is a mistake. All you can do is prepare your daughter for the world; eventually you must let her live in it.

The first man a woman loves sets the tone for her life. Therefore, it is my job as a parent to make sure that my daughter will not be held up by my rules or by my desire to have her end this process any earlier than the moment she finds a good man. What most parents fail to realize is that these days, this search has become a lot harder. I would rather my daughter spend her late teens and much of her twenties dating as many men as possible than tell her she cannot date at all or that she is supposed to only date one person.

I will not be fearful of the choices she will make, because she will have had sixteen to seventeen years' worth of parenting to protect her from peer pressure. I will tell her that any effort she puts in before marriage should not be put into one person. The effort should be put into the process of finding the one person. To some this may seem strange, but you have to ask yourself, can a woman do both?

Can a woman be a good woman to a man, and at the same time, find the best possible man to be good to? If not, then which one will you choose?

You Must Be Ready

When a real man comes for you
When the sex is just the icing
on the cake of what
he wants from you.
When loving you is what he wants to do.
If your goal is to one day be mother and wife,
You must first remove
all of these demons from your life.
Start tonight.
Start with the people who have been
in your corner for so long,
But still expect you to fight.
Finish with the ones who only had your back
long enough
To find a place to plant the knife.
Tell them, "It's life." Tell them you're finished.
Tell them you're done trying to convince
someone they're a winner.
Tell them, "It's dinner."
And you'd rather eat alone
Before you ever prepare a place for someone
Who hasn't proven that they belong.
If it's no longer music to your ears, change the song.
Tell them you're tired.
Tell them you've got to let go of the things
that weigh you down
So you can go higher.
No more liars. Live, and let live.
If not for yourself,
Do it for the thoughts that keep you up at night
About how you want to be married with kids.

Do it for the husband in your head.
Do it for the desire to experience true love at least once
Before you're dead.
If not, quit now.
Put a "For Sale" sign up on your future and your crown.

When They Ask Me Why I'm Single

I'll tell 'em.
There's a woman.
Beautiful.
From calcaneus to crown.
But right now,
She's got a boyfriend.
But she also hasn't been happy in months.
And she tells me all the time
That if it wasn't for her son,
We'd be something.
I'll tell 'em that
Every twenty-seven seconds
A woman gets beat
to the point of shedding blood—
Not by strangers,
But by the people she loves.
And sometimes it's their boyfriends.
And sometimes they don't leave after.
Some of these women didn't need boyfriends,
They needed pastors.
When they ask me why I'm single,
I'll tell 'em:
Some women stood for something...
Then met a man who gave them everything...
But it came with a price.
She could never be his wife.
Because he already had one.
And she was down with it.
I guess when you worship anything long enough

it becomes a religion.
When they ask me why I'm single,
I'll tell 'em
There's a woman right now
Who's on round four with him,
And she's down three to nothing.
But she thinks the fact that he keeps coming back
means something.
I keep trying to tell her that it doesn't,
But she's got me stored in her phone as her cousin.
So…that doesn't look promising.
I'll tell them that fear keeps
more prisoners than love ever will.
And some women will never chill,
Because he's got her schedule on ice,
And in my life,
I've never seen a woman worthier of her freedom.
Girl, you know you don't need him.
I'm single because
there's a woman in this room,
And as bad as she wants to jump the broom,
She won't.
And I respect her too much to call her a punk.
But at the same time,
She doesn't call me at all,
All because some other dude didn't catch her
after he made her fall.
There's a difference between hating
And wanting women to want better
Than these silly rabbits
Who will try to assassinate your character
for some carrots.
Who try to tell you that you're average
Because they don't know diamond.

There is no such thing as bad timing,
Only people who are bad with time.
And if you had a dad you would been fine.
But even fathers aren't what they used to be.
If you ever knew love once,
Chase it.
Daily, like a fiend. Nightly like a dream.
But always like a Queen.

You are smart
You are beautiful
You are important.
But more important,
You are woman.
The second attempt at human.
Proof that,
Even after man,
There was still
Room for improvement.
If anybody tells you different,
Tell them to prove it.

TEN THINGS EVERY WOMAN MUST NEVER FORGET

1. The woman you are will never be measured by how many men are interested, but by how well you learn to separate the interested from the eligible.

2. Never apologize for your wall. The lazy will complain. The strong will too—just from the other side.

3. Love will leave you in some strange places; the beauty is learning how to make a strange place home.

4. It's okay to be lonely, it's okay be in love, just never both at the same time.

5. Whenever you feel like you're asking for too much, remember that you are a queen, and every queen lives in a castle. Only two types of people are allowed in that castle: the king, and the help.

6. It's pointless to lose sleep over people you don't wake up with.

7. Sometimes you have to pull the car over and let some people out, when it's clear that the two of you aren't going in the same direction.

8. There are going to be a million things you'll die without knowing. Don't let one of them be yourself.

9. Let "happiness" be a party at your house. And the only people invited are the ones who like your music.

10. If you expect the world to be fair with you, because you're fair with it, quit now. Just surround yourself with enough people willing to listen to you complain.

The Perfect Boyfriend Tour

In January of 2016, I decided that I wanted to go on tour again. But when I listened to the feedback from my poetry shows, it was brought to my attention that there never seemed to be enough time to actually sit down and talk to the women. When I travel and speak, I always pride myself in being visible until the last person leaves the venue, no matter how long it takes, how many books I'll have to sign, or how many pictures I will take with them. I feel that I at least owe it to these women, who even though they have never seen me before this night, have at times made life-changing decisions based on my words. Spending a few extra minutes is going the extra mile. So that's what I was doing, but I noticed that it still wasn't enough for some women.

I felt that for my next tour, I wanted to do something more intimate. I feel that a lot of the poetry that I write and perform leaves women with questions. I wanted to develop a place where I could answer some of those questions. I wanted it to be in a place where women could feel safe. So, I decided to go on The Perfect Boyfriend Tour.

I went to five different cities: Houston, Atlanta, New York, Los Angeles, and Miami —don't worry, more cities will be added!—and I invited fifteen women at a time to a home that I rented, where I prepared a meal for them, and then I sat and I talked with them. I knew that my book was going to be called *The Boyfriend Book*, but as I said previously, I didn't know necessarily whether it was going to be a book about what love is supposed to feel like from a boyfriend, or whether or not you even needed a boyfriend at all. I decided I would let this tour be the determining factor.

I ended up selling out in all of the cities, and there were approximately three hundred women who showed up. The youngest was sixteen and the oldest was fifty-five, but they all had one common thread: their unsuccessful search for love and how it had left them.

So I put together an outline that walked women through from the beginning to the end, from single to married. As we broke this timeline of a woman's journey down into smaller parts and we tried to figure out where a boyfriend would fit, we quickly realized that he didn't.

Transparency

I had a girlfriend before, and I enjoyed the fact that I had something that was mine. Actually, I was fortunate enough to be in four relationships with four totally different but totally amazing women. The sad part is, I don't speak to any of them anymore. We aren't enemies, but we aren't friends. On one hand I feel frustrated and disappointed. These were the people to whom I got the closest, the ones with whom I shared my biggest dreams and my scariest nightmares. At one point, these were the people that I thought I was going to spend the rest of my life with. So, after those people were taken away, part of me is left feeling like it was all a waste of time. But luckily, I am wise enough to get it: that when you really do love somebody and it doesn't work, sometimes you have no choice but to be strangers. That doesn't mean you hate them; it means that maybe you can't go from being on the inside to being on the outside looking in. The frustrating part is that while I appreciate the journey we went through, no matter how I tell the story, it still ends.

So now the question is, "Who gets the blame?" First, blame is a tricky word. It is used to determine fault or responsibility for something wrong. Now, I wouldn't go as far as saying that any woman who ever had a boyfriend who didn't eventually become her husband made a mistake, but I would argue that some women spend a lot of time sticking around, trying to breathe life into dead situations. So I sat and I thought to myself, how can we can fix it? I did some more research. The average relationship lasts two years and nine months. The average woman starts dating at seventeen. The average woman wants to be married at twenty-nine.

I used to think the problem was that there weren't enough good men to go around. What I'm discovering is that not enough women are single long enough to find them. The average woman is only single for six to ten months in between relationships. This makes me question the point of being in relationships at all. From the perspective of time, it just doesn't make sense, especially in cases like mine. I spent three years with one woman, four years with another, and two women got a year of my time—all exclusively. So mathematically, I gave nine good years of my life to a bunch of women who probably will never be my wife. Now I'm sitting here at thirty-one, just as single as I was at seventeen, without much to show for it but some lessons and a heart that has become a lot better at healing itself. While I'm grateful, that's still not a lot to show for nine years of hard work. Maybe my grandmother was right.

Recent Trend in Marital Status of U.S. Adults, Ages 18 to 29

■ % Currently married   ■ % Single/Never married   ■ % Living with partner

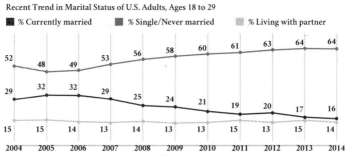

Based on combined Gallup nationwide cross-sectional polls conducted each year
GALLUP

SHELTER

You won't know who's for you
until you're at your worst.
Beaten. Black and Blue.
Heart broken in two,
Too solid to sew, too heavy for glue.
It is then that all those lonely nights
will come to an end
And he'll love you till it hurts.
Gentleman enough to put you first.
Yet humble enough to put in the work.
And his life will revolve around you
Like the sun that you are.
Opening your eyes, heart,
and the door to your car.
And he's not far.
Just on the other side of your comfort zone.
Where the sacrifice for waiting
for something that still feels good
in the morning
Might mean a couple of nights alone.
You won't know who could love you
Until the moments in your life
when you don't love you.
Until you have to rely on their positive energy
to keep you alive and away from your enemies.
Some place safe and warm.
Out of the rain, and away from the storm.
He's coming.
Your knight in shining armor.
Half hero. Half farmer.
Ready to help you lace your boots.

Willing to fix you at your roots.
So, you'll grow.
So, you'll know that any man can love you
when you're okay.
But the real ones will realize that you're not,
…and still stay.

The Struggle

For me, the beauty in being the type of writer that I am is that it has united women—women from different backgrounds, countries, and cultures, all tied together for one common agenda: empowerment. I feared that this book would drive a wedge between these women, and the last thing I want to do is divide women since women are strongest when they are together.

On one hand, I had this concept for a book where all I did was write love letters to women; letters that gave women hope, peace, love, and respect—all the things that a good "boyfriend" was supposed to do. On the other hand, I had this new knowledge about boyfriends. This new knowledge didn't necessarily agree with my new book, and if I wasn't careful, I would only be perpetuating the same monster that has destroyed so many women's lives, this "monster" being the current state of "boyfriend" and "girlfriend."

Part of me wishes that I didn't know what I know or feel what I feel on the inside. I understand now what people mean when they say ignorance is bliss. I am painted into a corner. I have this knowledge, and I also have a following of women who listen to me. This makes me very cautious about the vibes I create, the energy I give out, and the words that I put into the universe.

To expect every woman to read this book and say, "You know what, I don't ever want a boyfriend again" would be almost impossible. For some women, all they know is boyfriend. Some women have boyfriends as we speak. In their defense, they could be some of the best boyfriends around. It would be unfair for me to use my platform and my voice to try and break up happy homes. I promise that isn't my goal.

My goal is to give you a book about the facts, and maybe a little of my opinion about the facts, so that you have a complete, but more importantly, an impartial view about what a boyfriend is and what a boyfriend isn't. After that, the choice is yours. The only advice I can give you moving forward is to make sure that regardless of whom the choice may help and whom it may hurt, always make sure the choice is 100 percent yours.

The Truth

No matter how badly you want to believe that on the back of your birth certificate there is a marriage certificate with your name already filled in, just waiting for the day you find your king, that is not the case. Three hundred thousand women are going to die this year without having ever been married. For some of these women, marriage was their ultimate goal, so my question is: were these women's lives failures because they never married?

Granted, some of these women will die young, but some of them won't. Some of them will have lived long, productive, amazing lives, but just could never find the one person who was both willing and worthy to help them achieve this goal.

So I want to use this moment as an opportunity to really challenge you about what your goals are. Nobody has the luxury of knowing that they're going to be around forever. So, what I want every person who reads this to understand is that if tomorrow itself is not promised, how can any woman honestly believe that these things—marriage, family, and being in love—are? Especially when so much of the responsibility for completing these goals lies in the hands of someone else?

We have become a people so captivated by love that we forget that love is not promised. We forget that each of us has a life independent of everyone else. Marriage is not success. Marriage is marriage. Society has done an amazing job making us believe that marriage and family are the "dream," but too many people chase that dream and end up in a nightmare. So, if you're the type of person who thinks success looks like something that involves a "plus one," then I think you need to reevaluate your happiness.

So, I challenge you to remove the thought of being a wife as a goal of yours. At first, it may seem a bit devastating to do, but as you grow, you'll notice that this is your best defense against "bad love" and disappointment. And what it will also do is put you in a position to conquer some of the other goals that you may have for yourself.

Think of your life this way: unless you become famous enough that the world will mourn your death, or unless you leave a legacy powerful enough that they will still write about the work you have done even after you leave this earth, then all you will have to document your presence here is your obituary.

What will it look like if you don't get married? What will it say if it doesn't say mother, or even wife? You have an obligation to set a course for your life from beginning to end, that does not involve the presence of someone else for your goals to be fulfilled. And you are to walk in this purpose, unbothered, until the day a man convinces you to do otherwise.

HIM

What scares me is that sometimes,
The only thing standing
between me and a good woman
Is her boyfriend.
And she's loyal.
To a fault.
More loyal to him than to her heart.
And it makes me smile, but it makes me wonder.
What kind of rules are we living under?
Too many men
Have the woman of my dreams in their bed,
And won't even roll over and kiss her goodnight for me.
Will probably never make her a wife for me.
So, for the life of me,
I can't understand why this man
Gets the pleasure of you exclusively.
The race a woman runs does not stop for any man.
It stops at the end.
If he is a boy, and I am a man,
Why can't we both be your friends?
Pressure bursts pipes.
It also makes comfortable boyfriends act right.
What scares me is that sometimes,
The only thing standing
between me and a good woman
Is the "not so good man" who met her before I did.
Who took her off the market
Before she could calculate her worth.
So, she never knew that true love
wasn't supposed to hurt.
So, she stayed. Never packed. Always prayed.

Hoping that God would give her a sign.
That this relationship
wasn't just a three-year waste of time.
To her, I say,
Sometimes God won't move until you do.

Love or People

Okay, so let's bring it back to the top. Ultimately, if we've come to the agreement that marriage is not guaranteed, and that the ultimate goal in life should be happiness, then what is the relationship between happiness and commitment? If the ultimate goal is happiness, pursuing happiness should be above all else, right? That means whether you're by yourself or with the "love of your life," your goal is to be happy. So what happens when happiness doesn't match up with commitment? What do you do?

There is no such thing as
"the love of your life."
There is only
"the person you love today,"
And the hope it
lasts forever.

When I was in a room with these women on this tour, I asked them. First, we said that the ultimate goal was happiness. Then some women challenged me and said that the ultimate happiness would be marriage. They said, "Yes, we all want happiness," but we all agreed that if they could get married to their "perfect boyfriend," then the ultimate goal would be marriage.

Then they all shared their beliefs about marriage. All of them were pretty different. Some women wanted to be housewives, some women wanted their husbands to stay home, but they all shared the one common thread of "the rest of your life."

So to challenge their thinking, I offered these women two scenarios.

First, let's say you're the average woman. Statistics say the average woman wants to get married at twenty-nine. Statistics also say that your average woman lives to be about eighty-three.

Let's say you're an average woman and you get married at twenty-eight, and you believe in commitment, so you would stay married until age eighty-three. That's fifty-five years, God and good health willing, with the same man. If only it could be so simple. Let's say I knock on your door tomorrow. To my right I have one man, and to my left, I've got three men. Then, I offer you two options. I say, "To my right is your husband, and he loves you very, very much, and for the next fifty years of your life, no matter what you go through, he will never leave you. But the price you must pay for him never leaving is him breaking your heart."

And when I say, "breaking your heart," I'm not talking about burning the bacon or forgetting to pick the kids up from school. When I say, "He's going to break your heart," I mean he's going to do those things that no woman could ever want her husband to do. Whatever the one thing is that a man could do that could hurt you, that one thing you ask him, "Please, never do this," he does that. And let's say he does it twice, but he never leaves.

Then, I tell you that on my left, I have three different men. One of them you could take home today, and the other two you're going to meet at other parts of your life. So, from twenty-eight to forty, you would spend every day of your life with one man, and you'll be as happy as a single mom with an overnight babysitter who likes to clean, too. You two will travel the world and make good love, great memories, and beautiful babies. Until the day he hurts you that one time, and after that one time, you'll pick your happiness over this commitment and you'll leave.

Then, at some date to be determined, you'll meet the second man, and you will share twenty beautiful years together with him, twenty years of happiness and commitment, and then somewhere along the way, the commitment will have to end. And as much as you do not want to throw away twenty years' worth of love, you promised yourself never to let your history get in the way of your future, so you will leave.

"Love isn't a thing you've got to do
before you turn thirty-five.
So, if you think you're racing a clock,
that's the worse frame of mind
that you would ever want
to be in as a woman.
Because now you're
chasing the clock and these guys,
and that's something you
don't ever want to do."

Now you're sixty, and after you've gone through your second divorce, you fly down to Florida to be with your daughter. And two doors down from her is a man who's about your age. He's also had a point or two in his life where he had to choose between his happiness and his commitment, and he made the same tough decisions you did. The next thing you know, you see him at bingo, you two get to talking, and not long after, you two are riding off into the sunset together. And you'll spend the rest of your days together, cherishing the years you have left.

So which type of woman would you want to be? Would you want to be that woman who said, "You know what, Mike? I've got my one guy, and he never left me for sixty years. Now, he broke my heart, but he never left." Or do you want to be this other woman? Do you want to be this woman who picked three guys but had near-constant happiness? She had to renew her commitments, but she was always happy.

And I believe that. Before I can even talk to you about why I think you shouldn't have a boyfriend again, I have to know where you stand on happiness as it pertains to commitment and as it pertains to love, because you've got to love yourself enough to pick happiness over commitment. You have to love yourself enough to pick happiness over people. Or else none of this is going to work.

*"Never let who they are
mean more than how they fit,
because no matter
who the relations are with,
it is still your ship."*

Time

I know the thought of being thirty and single is scary.
But you could have been twenty-seven with a baby.
And instead of him driving you to work,
he's driving you crazy.
And the nights could be longer than the days.
And your hair could have less shine and more grays.
And you could still not be in love.
Because you thought that being happy
was being married.
So you did it early.
Only to spend as much money
as you spent on the wedding
On an attorney.
When the whole time,
you missed the beauty of the search,
The excitement of a phone book full of men
ready to put in work.
Your problem is,
You've got this clock around your heart that ticks.
Like happiness is a party that,
if you're not dressed in time, you'll miss.
If that's how you feel, dig a ditch and bury yourself.
And before you ever settle, marry yourself.
But what you're not going to do is rush the process.
I know what you're feeling.
You just want it to be over.
You're tired of giving your all just to get back half.
But you can't drop out of school
just because you hate math.
The more exotic the destination,
The tougher the path.

You just make sure you make it.
Because the alternative is to fake it.
And life's already too much work for you to sweat it.
So before you buy it, be sure that you love it.
And the next time you get nervous,
Wondering how long until you get
the wedding bells and churches,
Remember that you can't rush the plan,
And you damn sure can't rush a man.
But when he comes,
The wait will be well worth it.

Misunderstood

In life, be very careful about people who introduce problems to you without a solution. The problem here is boyfriend. The solution is where I need your help. We live in a time where we want everything and we want it now, from the creation of fast food, to overnight shipping, to love. In some ways we have made the world a better place. In others, we have handicapped the beauty and the memories that come with patience. Let's use boyfriend as an example.

Before boyfriend, there was courting. The cool thing for men about courting was that we had the ability, the option, and the free will to court as many women as we liked. For women, it allowed them to be courted in the same manner. I wasn't around when the process began, but from what I've read, at some point, some man decided that he didn't want to go through the competition of courting the same woman some other man was pursuing. Without going into great detail, ultimately, the title of "boyfriend" was born. With it came the option to bypass the sometimes years-long process of courting. In return, we got the proverbial ninety-day rule. After ninety days, we feel that we have seen enough to be able to commit to someone. And it gets worse.

Furthermore, even beyond the expectation of speeding up the courtship process, they handicapped the competition process. So now, not only is a woman supposed to speed up the courting, but she must also isolate herself from every other man who is interested. I don't understand how women win here. So, when I say eliminate boyfriend, what are you really losing?

Think of it this way. The way relationships are set up now, picture a woman, single and ready to mingle. She makes herself available to the dating and courtship process. She makes it known that she is at a point in her life where she is ready for love, commitment, etc. So, she begins to have a line of interested candidates form at her front gates. They will all be outside, dressed to the best of their ability, smelling great, looking good, with their game faces on, ready to prove that they are the one. Since the creation of boyfriend, now men have the ability to question how long they have to sit outside "with everybody else" waiting for her to choose. A woman, feeling the pressure, is sometimes forced to make a decision. So what she does is pick the best possible candidate, open her gate, and allow him, and only him, in.

Now, on the inside, it's only him, while everyone else is on the outside.

Then he has no competition. The same man who was just outside begging for an opportunity now has the entitlement of expectation. That's a lot of privilege for someone who has only put in a couple weeks or months of effort. Now, he feels some sense of security. Security turns into comfort. Comfort turns into relaxation. Before you know it, he's done trying to impress you. Before you get mad at him, I need you to realize that you are the one who gave him this sense of security in the first place. So who should you really be mad at, you or him?

So, what's the alternative? Patience. Let's say that instead of the men lining up in front of your door, they are at the foot of a mountain. At the top there is you, unbothered and patient. At the bottom of the mountain, there is no gate, just a sign—a sign that says enter at your own risk.

Any man interested in the position is free to enter. This will begin the race that every woman should witness before she closes her gate. Not all men will make it to the top, but they will all have an equal opportunity to try. Some will start off strong, some will finish strong, but only one will make it to the top. My challenge to you is not to make it easy for any of them, but only to be a witness. What you will discover is the beauty of watching men compete for you. This is necessary both for your safety and your self-esteem. There is only so long that people can pretend. Eventually the weak, the lazy, and the impatient will all quit. That's fine. They aren't the ones you wanted anyway. Like I said, not everyone who starts will finish. What you will figure out about yourself and about love is that you won't care. All you needed was one to finish anyway. When you have a boyfriend, though, it kind of handicaps your ability to not care as much.

Why? Because instead of sitting at the top of the mountain, unbothered by one man dropping out, you are now fighting to keep the person you picked on the inside. Why? Because he is your boyfriend, and you just turned everyone else away.

WHATEVER YOU DO

Don't stop believing.
First, in yourself.
Second, in love.
Third, in a mixture of the two
That will give you a new definition of what happy is.
Believe that you'll never flinch,
When a 3 a.m. argument
Has you at the fork in the road
between being happy, and being "his."
Believe in kids.
Believe in Reciprocity. Monogamy. Marriage. Family.
Believe that all those flaws,
in the hands of a real man,
will just be candy.
And he'll swallow you whole,
And the first thing he'll want to get inside of is your soul.
It is then that you'll discover
That there's a thin line between
Being "in love" and "out of control."
Believe that you're worth every penny that you desire.
Believe that there's still a good woman in there somewhere.
You're just waiting for the right man to light the fire.
Sometimes all you're left with is your beliefs.
And they'll be the determining factor
of whether you're going to lose
people or sleep.
Choose people.
Because the bags always look better under your arms
than under your eyes.
And you're never too young to love, or too old to cry.
Expect the truth. Accept the lies.

Only then will you fly.
And, hopefully, you'll end up in the arms of a man.
Who has both your best interest at heart, and a plan.
If you do that
I believe you'll be happy in the end

A woman
who walks
in her own purpose
will never need direction,
only company.

The Road

Let's recap. We've agreed that marriage is not promised, but it is possible. Okay. So now all we've got to do is figure out how to get married. Easier said than done! I wish I could write a book about how to get married, because if I could, I would read it myself and I'd be married. So for now, you have to trust me. I know it's so hard to take advice on how to get married from a guy who's not married, but hear me out.

Simple question: Can a woman get married without having a boyfriend?

At first, when I asked people, everybody would tell me no. To be honest, if you'd have asked *me* five years ago, I might have told you no, too. I guess what gets a lot of women nervous is that when they think about love, happiness, and all of this family stuff, they think about it having to last "the rest of their lives," and they get overwhelmed. Forget forever for now. Forever could end up only being until tomorrow. I want to talk to you about today; today--until the day some man decides that you are too valuable to his life for him to ever go another day without you. How do you get from one point to the other?

The easy answer would be boyfriend. The problem is I don't believe in this word, especially not the way it's being used today. Boyfriend turns "option" into "obligation." I believe that the word should be removed from the English dictionary. I most certainly don't believe that it is a requirement for women who want to one day be married. If the only argument people can give me is that "It has worked for over a hundred years, and no one has done anything about it," to those people I say, the word "boyfriend" was first used in 1910, and it wasn't added to the Webster's dictionary until 1918.

So, if you're looking for evidence, here's 1,900 years' worth of proof that there were some people who got from single to married without the need for boyfriend. Because it never existed.

Now I know what you're thinking, it's 2016, so things have to be different. Okay, so you want different? Here's different. How about a different view on this road from single to married? Conventional relationship people will tell you all right, as a woman, you meet a man. You show him enough of you that he likes you. You get into a relationship with him. Y'all do that for a while. But let me ask you this question: Could boyfriend ever be the end for you? Could you ever be solely satisfied by just a boyfriend? I don't know too many women who are like that.

I don't know too many women who would be okay if their journey just stopped at boyfriend.

So if we agree that we could never allow ourselves and our journeys to stop at boyfriend, then my question to you is, why should it start there? Now, I know what you're thinking, and I've been thinking the same thing, too. As a woman, can you really expect a man to commit to you and ask you to marry him without you being his girlfriend first?

I knew it. What if I told you that you were asking the wrong question? We don't have to answer that question of whether or not the whole world's going to do it. We are not here looking to marry the whole world. We are looking for that one person with whom we can run away from the world—the one person with whom we can build our own world.

The real question is, do you believe in it? Enough to execute it every day of your life? Even when it hurts? Even when you think you might be close? If the answer is yes, then the ball is and will forever be in your court.

If you constantly
Require a man to be
by your side,
How can you ever
be seen as an entrée.
Boyfriend is a hotel
on the side of the road
Between
Single and fiancée.
So, before you go pulling over
And getting a room
Because you think
you're grown,
Make sure you're lying down with a man
who's willing to take you home.

SAFE

In a world where every woman
Feels like she has to be just a little bit prettier,
A little bit skinnier,
A little bit stronger,
A little more perfect,
A little less real,
She needs a man.
A man with arms like water.
Soft enough to wash away her insecurities,
But strong enough to carry her burdens.
With hands like German shepherds.
Big enough to bury her face in when she can't keep it
together,
But loyal enough to never turn against her.
His lips are like cotton.
Soft enough to kiss her most fragile of parts.
But strong enough to speak confidence into her soul.
It is with this man
That she will be her unapologetic self.
Where three extra pounds
are just an opportunity to love you three times as much,
Where three bumps on your face are only proof that God
is still
Working on the masterpiece he calls your beauty.
Where stretch marks are tiger stripes to scare away any
man who
Can't handle a woman who's still growing.
Where her tears aren't a reason for you to run.
But a confirmation that she feels comfortable enough
around you
To let her guard down.

There is no greater peace than coming home to a sense of
security.
Knowing that you're safe.
Because the man at the door is in love with the woman
in the mirror.
It is at this moment
Everything will become clearer.
That just as much as home is a place,
It's a person.

Wedding Day vs. Engagement

So, let's talk about marriage. Marriage is your wedding day. That's the day that you and he invite all of your friends, all of your family, and maybe even some people you don't know that well, if you think they are going to buy nice gifts (petty, but honest). Symbolically, it is the opportunity for you to allow other people to witness the day that you two agree before God that you have chosen to "do life together." My question to you is: didn't this day kind of happen already?

At some point prior to that day, you had your engagement day. Now, since I'm always trying to have women question the things they think they know, let me talk to you again. Let me ask you this question about engagement.

Which is the more important day in your life? Is it your engagement day, or the day you get married? I really want you to think about these two days very hard before you answer. Which day is more emotionally important to you? I say that it's your engagement day, and here's my thinking.

Ultimately, no matter how much you may love a man, you can never ever make a man do anything he doesn't want to, and even if you could, you shouldn't want to do that. This includes making him get down on one knee and asking you to be his wife. What more women need to realize is that the true measure of what type of man you have is the type of plan that he has for you. So if you never "pressured" a man to be anything to you or for you except to be himself, and he still went out and bought you a ring and asked you for forever: what day is more important than that?

Your wedding day? You want to know how I feel about a wedding day? The same way I feel about Christmas—something that started off so simple that turns into something so ridiculous that sometimes I don't want to bother.

On a good day, I feel like the creation of the wedding was a woman's opportunity for a do-over—a very, very, very, very expensive do-over. As I'm writing this, I'm wondering if I will be able to use this theory on my wife, and then maybe we won't have to have a wedding.

The basic requirements of a wedding, whether we are talking legally or religiously, are a woman in a nice outfit, a witness, a ring, some religious figure, and me, of course—i.e., the groom. If this is true, then all I have to do is take you out to dinner someplace nice and propose to you after dessert, and then we're technically married. Why do we need to spend thirty thousand dollars (Google it) so you can make sure everybody's there? I mean you already said yes, so unless you plan on changing your answer, let's save the money for the kids' college fund! (Also, thirty thousand dollars! Can someone say scholarships!)

And if she wanted something a little more poetic, I would say, "When I propose to you, when any man proposes to any woman, it will be because she is the most beautiful woman he has ever met. Which means whatever she is wearing that day would be perfect. Then all we need is a witness, so whether it's the waiter or the twenty thousand other people at the basketball game, we will have what we need. Technically, it could just be you, me, God, and a four carat pear-shaped yellow diamond (Dream big, ladies), and all the requirements would be filled."

The only thing a wedding does is give you the opportunity to steal my spotlight. You get to get your hair done, you're in this super expensive dress, and you invited all your girlfriends, most of whom either I don't like or they don't like me, and since you knew in advance this time, they even gave you a ring to give me back. That's just rude and insensitive. So, my vote is, let's live-stream the whole engagement and be done with it. People buy crappy gifts these days anyway.

Maybe I'll tell her we can use the money we would have spent on the wedding and she can buy her own gifts.

HERE ARE TEN WEDDING FACTS THAT MOST WOMEN PROBABLY DON'T KNOW

1. Engagement and wedding rings are worn on the fourth finger of the left hand because it was once thought that a vein in that finger led directly to the heart. (Which is not true. Google "Vena Amoris.")

2. Queen Victoria is credited with starting the Western world's white wedding dress trend in 1840—before then, a bride simply wore her best dress. (The average cost of a wedding dress as of 2017 was $1,509.)

3. If your bridesmaids are less than thrilled about matching dresses, tell them they're good luck! The tradition of matching maids dates back to Roman times, when people believed evil spirits would attend the wedding in an attempt to curse the bride and

groom. Bridesmaids were required to dress exactly like the bride in order to confuse the spirits and bring luck to the marriage.

4. On a similar note, brides traditionally wear veils because ancient Greeks and Romans believed veils protected brides from evil spirits.

5. The tradition of a bride wearing "something old, something new, something borrowed, and something blue" comes from an Old English rhyme. Something old represents continuity; something new offers optimism for the future; something borrowed symbolizes borrowed happiness; and something blue stands for purity, love, and fidelity.

6. The tradition of a wedding cake comes from ancient Rome, where guests broke a loaf of bread over the bride's head for fertility's sake.

7. Ever wondered where the phrase "tying the knot" came from? In many cultures around the world— including Celtic, Hindu, and Egyptian—the hands of the bride and groom are literally tied together during their wedding to demonstrate the couple's commitment to each other and their new bond.

8. If you thought we were over the spirit thing, think again. According to tradition, the groom carries the bride across the threshold to valiantly protect her from evil spirits lurking below.

9. June weddings are not a new thing. The Roman goddess Juno rules over marriage and childbirth, hence the popularity of June weddings.

10. Honeymoons weren't always so luxurious. Ancient Norse bridal couples went into hiding after the wedding, and a family member would bring them a cup of honey wine for thirty days—or one moon, which is how the term "honeymoon" originated.

POWER

Boyfriend.
When done right,
I heard he's supposed to turn "girlfriend" into "wife."
And if I'm understanding it right,
At some point,
He's the only man allowed in your life.
And as a woman,
The only thing you're supposed to do is sit and wait.
For this man to decide
If he wants to pay for the food he just ate.
But you've been feeding him since the beginning.
Hoping that keeping him happy now,
Letting him taste the milk before he buys the cow,
Will somehow get you walking down the aisle.
If this is the truth,
Then a lot more than toast is going to be burned in these
kitchens.
If I were a woman, I would be nervous.
Because to me,
It sounds like you could be perfect,
But you won't make it to the altar of any of them churches
Until he thinks you deserve it.
Until he thinks you put enough work in.
You could end up giving the best years of your body
To a man who may only see you as a hobby.
Now, I understand why women care so much about the
ring.
Without it, nothing you do for him means a thing.
So I hope you get it.
Because, until then
Every part of yourself that you feed him,

Is on credit.
So make sure you're keeping your receipts.

Exclusive

Have you ever liked something so much that you wanted it all to yourself? Have you ever liked yourself so much that you only wanted to give you to one person? Me too. By nature, we are a stingy people. We are possessive about everything, especially our lovers. Sometimes, this possessiveness comes before the "purchase."

People want to take you off the market before they pay. So, the only real question is, when should we be exclusive? When does a man have the right to tell you that he is the only person you can like? When can he tell you that he is the only person for whom you can make time? I say, when that man asks you to be his wife. He might say it's when he calls you "girlfriend." Ultimately, though, it's up to you.

If you are about to give this man a role—the role—as the co-star in the major motion picture that is the rest of your life, that must have been one hell of an audition. If not, ask for more. But is that enough to stop you from what your purpose was before he showed up? Is being his "girlfriend" enough insurance to make you put all your eggs in one basket? In the dictionary, boyfriend does not say "exclusive." Does that mean that you should never be exclusive to any man that isn't your husband?

One of my biggest problems with the idea of how you are with a boyfriend is that it's too much like being a wife. The problem is, it hardly comes with the investments a man is supposed to make for his wife, but almost always has the obligations a man would ask *of* his wife. This boyfriend thing is a man, seeing a woman out here conquering life and taking no prisoners—only to make her a prisoner of his own.

A woman who understands the value of having a good man will never jeopardize her integrity or her journey by allowing just any man to "be in the way."

Your boyfriend could very well be your future husband. He could also be something much worse. Boyfriend is like layaway for some women. It is the biggest IOU a woman can allow a man to write. It's like a man walking into a store, seeing something he likes, and getting permission to place it on hold. Then no one else can touch it, feel it, or love it enough to take it home today.

Unfortunately, some men never make it back to the store; others take forever to pay. And all women suffer because of it.

Practice

During the Miami leg of the tour, there was a young lady aged eighteen who told me that she liked the idea of having a boyfriend. She said, "It would be good practice for the real thing." I told her, "You cannot practice love, only experience it, and I'm pretty sure you don't want anything less than love, so what are you practicing?"

She replied, "Well, how can I experience love if I don't try to fall in it?" I told her, "Baby girl, you *are* love. So, fall in yourself. Before you ever fall for a man, you must witness him preparing a place for you to land."

I think about how many other women think like her. So many women are so in a rush to give some of the best years of their lives away—for practice. I asked her how much practice she thought she needed. She smiled and said, "A lot." Then I made her an offer: I told her I would let her have her practice if she agreed to always practice with at least two people at the same time. She refused. She told me, "You can't give your all to two people at the same time." (Yes. She said, "your all." Meaning everything she's got. For practice. Not the actual game. But practice.) So before we iron out this "give your all" wrinkle in her armor, let's focus on the exclusive aspect.

If I had to pick my beefs with the concept of boyfriend, the biggest one is exclusivity. For some men, this is the one thing that they're scared to death about. I'm pretty sure some women are too. My question to you is, if that can be seen as one of the scariest things, since it eliminates the option for you to go elsewhere, how could you want to give that up for *practice*?

I've seen so many women throw so many valuable years away for boyfriends. You meet a guy when you're eighteen. You think he's the love of your life. You let him hang around until you're twenty-two. Then you realize that while some boys' bodies leave high school, their minds don't. And you've spent more practice years learning how to forgive, and then to forget. Then you meet another guy, and since you gave the last guy "your all," you probably fell "all the way in love" with that last guy.

Even though it ended, you were still bitten by the love bug, the most dangerous drug on earth. So, you want more love now, but you also want it faster, and, of course, better. You make it a point to go out and try to right your wrongs; you try to prove that it wasn't you, it was them. Don't you think both of you know that already?

Anyway, next thing you know, you're back at practice, this time at twenty-three. You try to find love and yourself... only to discover that you're behind. You're behind because you spent four years of your life at "practice," and then another year healing from your injuries, all for someone who never made it to the game.

Every woman
Should have a plan for life that doesn't
involve a man.
And this plan is what should wake her up
off of her pillow every morning.
She should be so consumed
With the phenomenal
womanhood

that is her existence,
So filled with passion
Toward perusing her purpose,
that anything less
Than amazing
Would be seen as nothing more
than a waste of time.

LAYAWAY

If you're not careful,
You'll give all of your good years to the game.
Only to sit on someone's bench.
Only for love to be a thirst,
That only one person is allowed to quench.
Please don't be one of those women
Who end up on some man's shelf…
One of those women
Who doesn't need a boyfriend,
But definitely needs help
Because she wonders why it keeps happening…
A man who sees your value, but can't pay today,
Who might not be ready right now, but still wants you to
stay.
Who expects you to compromise,
And you keep agreeing
To be girlfriend.
To be taken
Out of the window, and put in a box.
Taken to the back, with their name written on top,
"On hold for him."
Hoping he comes back with the balance.
Hoping he steps up to the challenge.
To fulfill his end of the bargain.
There are only two reasons a man makes you his girlfriend.
Because it's a good decision,
Or because he's nervous about a little competition.
So, if you don't do anything else, pay attention.
Keep your eyes and options open as long as you can.
If you play your cards right, you should end up with a man.
So, before you ever allow one to take you off the market,

Get in your car, drive somewhere far, and park it.
Get out, and ask yourself a question:
Am I loyal or lucky?
Because you could meet the man of your dreams
tomorrow,
And never get to wake up to him
Because you were taken
For granted.

Commitment

We are by nature a selfish people. As much as we want to believe that selfishness is our right, it is also a disease. To expect unselfishness from humans is truly a dangerous thing. We are such an unpredictable people; so weak in the flesh, so impatient, so greedy. It is almost certain that some people will fail. And, sometimes, you might be the one who they fail.

Yes, it's sad, but so is the fact that three million newborns die every year. You must remember, yes, sometimes people let you down, but sometimes you have them up too high. But I get it. I was it. I didn't have a job, a car, or a home, but I still wanted something that belonged to me. I wanted commitment. I still do, but what I have learned is that the only person I can truly expect it from is the one who promises God they will give that commitment to me…

I don't want you to get confused. I'm not saying two people should never commit to one another before they get married; I'm saying you shouldn't want them to. Life is about options. Relationships are about options. Before marriage, anything that we do should be independent of anybody else. Sometimes, you don't give people enough opportunity to show who they really are. How long do you get to actually witness who someone really is before you give him the responsibility of being your boyfriend?

Let's play a game. I was watching CNN one day, which I encourage everyone to do at least once a week for an hour. And it doesn't necessarily have to be CNN; it could be BBC, MSNBC, etc., but it is important to keep up with the world at least as much as you keep up with the Kardashians. I really don't pay much attention to their opinions, because the media makes you think what they want you to think. Anything pre-planned is not original. I just pay attention to the facts. And the fact is, this world is a dangerous place, which is even more of a reason for you to be careful of who you let into your place.

Anyway, they were talking about the president. They called him "The Leader of the Free World." All I thought was, damn; well, who's protecting him? Then I researched the Secret Service, which if you don't know, is the president's bodyguard detail. My thinking was that if he was the most important person in the world, then the most important job is protecting the most important person.

This is from their website:

> Candidates must be US citizens and must submit to urinalysis screening for illegal drug use prior to appointment. All Secret Service positions require a Top-Secret security clearance. All applicants must undergo a full, Secret Service-specific, Top-Secret clearance process regardless of current existing clearance standings; certain positions may also require the applicant to successfully complete a polygraph and/or medical examination. Age, vision, and excellent physical condition requirements may also apply.

And that was just to *qualify*. You still have to interview, pass the physical, and pass the mental examination. They check your credit as well as your credibility. I couldn't even get upset when they said the process may take up to five years. I completely understand their process. You must assign responsibility—responsibly. Furthermore, everyone knows what they are getting into before they sign up, and they proceed anyway.

I can only imagine how tough that road is. But when they get that call letting them know that they passed? I bet it's all worth it.

So of course, my question to you, Queen and leader of your own free world: how long does it take to get into your secret service? How thorough are your background checks? How much effort do you put in to test their physical and mental health? How long do you wait before you give someone the opportunity to be the one protecting you? Maybe the real question is, how good are you at protecting yourself until he shows up?

The best defense a woman has
is her standards.
They are the bars that will never break,
even when the men
who try to climb over them do.

Potential

You know what holds a lot of women back? Men who make more promises than progress. Not just any men, boyfriends. When a stranger or even someone you just casually date breaks a promise, it doesn't affect you too much, if at all. But when it's your "boyfriend," not only does it hurt more, but you don't even respond to it the same way. Being a boyfriend has bought many men time, but the only thing it has turned into in most cases is more time wasted.

In a day and age when so many women come across men who aren't even close, when a woman does encounter a man who even resembles what she's looking for out there, two things happen: comfort and compromise. This is a dangerous combination. Why? Because you'll start to get confused about what your purpose is. You have a responsibility to yourself to acquire the best possible candidate with whom to "do life." And you won't be able to do that if comfort and compromise have you waiting on someone's potential. In order to achieve in love, you must do two things. First, believe that what you seek exists. Second, be available to receive it. You can't do those things if you're still waiting for your boyfriend to reach his full potential.

Do you remember a movie called Willy Wonka and the Chocolate Factory? It's a pretty old film, so if you don't, the basic description of the movie goes like this. There was a chocolate factory owner who was going to invite a few lucky children to his factory, but you could only win an invitation if you purchased a candy bar that had a golden ticket on the inside. This excited the children so much that they would buy Willy Wonka chocolate with every penny they had in hopes that they would be the lucky one to find the golden ticket. The candy was no longer important, just being the lucky one to find the golden ticket on the inside.

Imagine if every man was a candy bar. Imagine if the golden ticket was love. Imagine if the factory was the dream home and the dream life you had planned well before you met this boyfriend. Imagine if your boyfriend wasn't a golden ticket, but a blue one.

Even though the blue ticket isn't gold, it's still better than opening up a candy bar and finding nothing on the inside. Attached to the ticket is a letter. So you read the letter, and it says that he knows how much you want a golden ticket. He goes on to admit that he isn't a golden ticket yet, but says he has the potential to be one, the same way your boyfriend tells you that he knows he has to try harder—the same way he tells you that he just needs more time and promises that he will be everything you need him to be. What do you do?

It's sad to say, but too many women are in relationships with blue tickets. The reason is because blue was better than nothing. The sad part is that sometimes, the ticket will never be anything more than blue.

This is why potential is so dangerous. So many women, through the course of their lives, open so many candy bars and find absolutely nothing. They attempt to give their time to a man, only for it to not even last beyond a second date. So when they do see something, even when it isn't necessarily what they were looking for, if it seems better than what they had, they start to question their journey. Do you know what you're supposed to do with that blue ticket? Appreciate it for its honesty. Because we all know that most men would grab some spray paint and try to be whatever color you're looking for. Then, you take that blue ticket, stick it on your refrigerator, go back to the store, and get yourself another candy bar.

Because like we said, the race a woman runs doesn't stop for any man, it stops at the end. So, you continue to search for your golden ticket. And if one day, that blue ticket does turn gold before you find one on your own, then so be it.

BIRD

I don't think you know how fly you are.
How much like "sky" you are.
For you to ever be in so deep that you drown.
For you to ever be head over heels for some clown
Whose idea of a good time
Is watching you play hide and go seek with your crown.
What happened to the woman who was here before him?
The one who made sure a man was qualified for the
position
Before she employed him?
If you weren't meant to see the world,
Then you wouldn't have wings.
If words were enough,
Then we wouldn't have rings.
But whichever you choose:
Matching tattoos,
Or a room full of family and friends when you say I do,
Don't get caught up in the "things."
You were meant to fly.
So, do so without apology.
And, wherever you may land,
Whether it be on a beach,
Or in the arms of a man,
Never change the plan,
Only the people.
And never fall in love with anything
less than your equal.
When you can't change the ending,
Write the sequel.
Faith
Is flying when broken.

Is leaving when hurting.
Is knowing
That one day you'll meet a man who's willing to fly too.

Prison

Some men control women even after it's over. Many women spend nine months recovering from nine-month relationships. Some never recover at all. Some have had their lives turned upside down because of a boy. The good news is that they got out. The bad news is that just like with anything else, it comes with a price. And that price for most women is some kind of wall.

You can't expect to escape love untouched. Everybody leaves, but everybody leaves something behind. For some women, it's a child. For others, it's a tattoo, it's a mortgage, it's the nightmares that still wake you up out of your sleep. For some women, it's not trying to love again. Those are the walls I'm scared of the most. Realize that every day that you're not growing, every day that you push the possibility of falling in love again down the road into the future, and every day that you're not getting better is a day when you're still in a relationship: with him.

I am a firm believer that the final part of the healing process is actually loving someone new. If you disagree, ask yourself, how can you know if you've fixed the leak unless you turn the water back on? Sometimes, this wall is holding you back from turning your water on. You meet a guy, and it doesn't work. And that changes the price of your rent by how much? That gives you how many extra sick days this year? By no means am I trying to trivialize your pain. You can hurt. If you've loved, you're supposed to hurt. Just do it while moving—further away from him, and closer to guys like me. And when our paths finally do cross, you can tell me about him; about how he had this queen and he blew it. And when you show me your wall, I'll be on the other side. And it will be because you gave me a ladder, or some rope—or some type of hope. Because if not, I'll never make it over. So the next time you ask yourself what's taking so long, when you wonder what's coming between you and the good man that you want so bad, make sure it isn't you and your wall.

Exit

When things don't add up,
May the first thing you subtract be yourself.
Because some men can be good for your body
but bad for your health.
Some will be everything you want but nothing you need.
But then again, sometimes dreams are just dreams.
Breaks from reality.
Where you won't lose because of a technicality.
Either way, every morning, God willing, the sun will rise.
And you're going to either have to put on your makeup
or a disguise.
And tell the world that this guy,
He's the best I can do.
As much as he is his own man, he's also a reflection of you.
So, choose your battles wisely.
You could spend the rest of your days
trying to turn the wrong man right,
And if you work hard enough, maybe you might.
Or you could find your Mr. Right
And jump to the part of the story when you're already a
wife.
The sad part is, the only thing holding you back isn't you.
No matter how many times you say you're happy, it isn't
true.
So how come it isn't through?
You're still fighting.
You find it easier to play and pretend than to be
enlightened.
And that thought has a man like me frightened.
We all make mistakes, some in the office, some on the
mattress.

But under no circumstances are you to tolerate the
madness.
Especially when it lives at your address
And causes you nothing but pain and sadness.
What a shame it is to fall in love with a cactus.
The majority of your relationships will just be practice.
So never be afraid to limit their expectations or their
access.
There is a good man waiting for you on the other side of
the atlas.
But first, you have to wrap up this joyride before it crashes.
Burn the bridge, spread the ashes.
In love, there is no award for best supporting actress.
If you need help, here are the matches.

If you were single,
then came across a man
you believed was
worthy enough to give your time to,
congratulations.
Don't follow that up with
the expectation for commitment
too soon.
Some women make a man
wait four months to be their girlfriend,
only to wait four years
for him to make her his wife.
Who is getting the better end of that deal?

Second Thoughts

The deeper I get into trying to identify what a woman's journey is, when I'm telling her not to have a boyfriend and not to be overly committed to the wrong kind of man, the more I start to get a little discouraged. It's easy for me, or for anyone else, to give advice on how we think you should live your life, but ultimately, only you are in the driver's seat. I'm afraid that the journey may be too long for some women to handle alone. This will result in their desire to acquire company. Society has taught us that the best way for a woman to do this is to get a boyfriend.

What I want you to understand is that when you become a girlfriend, a man takes the wheel—though not from a leadership or responsibility perspective. Women can most certainly lead. Most men would probably admit that their girlfriend is the better leader of the two anyway. What I mean is that when you become a man's girlfriend, it's now up to him whether or not you're going to get home. You leave your worth as well as the path for your life as it pertains to love in his hands—while you hope that he understands how much of a favor you did for him. And you hope he remembers that you picked him and allowed him to drive, allowed him to lead the two of you, and hoping he doesn't forget where he needs to take you: to the altar.

Another one of my major issues with boyfriends is the "commitment before the commitment" that it causes people to make. Sometimes, it puts women on layaway, and sometimes, they are set aside for men who never planned on coming back to pay in full. So when I meet women who swear that the only way to get married is to first become a girlfriend, I say that there must be a better way. Because, as a boyfriend, the only place this man can take you besides back home (while still single) is to a husband. So, if we talk about the process in terms of time and responsibilities, there is not enough equality.

The way things are now, two strangers meet, and more often than not, it's the woman who sets the bar. She does not allow herself to be conquered quickly, so she makes him put forth the effort to prove his interest. This continues until one of you starts worrying about what the other does when the two of you aren't together. It is from this fear that somebody will ask the other for some type of commitment. Before 1920, this would have meant he would have had to ask you to marry him. Or else it would have meant that the two of them would choose to commit to each other, as single people. These days, it means they can decide to be boyfriend and girlfriend. For all the women who think this change was in their favor, listen closely.

No Boyfriend, No Problem

The woman you are
Will not be defined by what type of man you have.
It will be defined by what type of plan you have.
Either you're going to be the woman who waits for the
right one,
Or the one who waits for her phone to go off
when the night comes.
You'll spend most of your time teaching,
But will it be teaching him how to get you into a white
dress,
Or how to get you out of a tight one?
The woman you are
Will be defined by how often you pick "self" over settle.
Too many women walk on eggshells for so long
They start feeling like rose petals.
So, it's my suggestion that you put yourself on a pedestal,
Closer to God. Away from the frauds.
It's the only way you'll ever stand out.
Because any woman who walks around with her hands out
Has to be prepared for what any man puts in them.
And you aren't taking any shortcuts anymore.
So whoever can't afford you
Will either admire us or ignore you.
But our price won't change.
And even if we are sad that we are single,
Our life won't change.
Because happiness is a party at our place.
So anyone invited that can't respect our space
Can take their talents anywhere they choose,

Just not in our face.

Respect the process.

Respect yourself enough to walk away from anything that doesn't

bring you peace, prosperity, or progress.

Everything else will work itself out.

Until then, the woman you are

Will always be faced with more issues

Than people around to solve them.

So, no excuses.

No losing.

No boyfriend.

No problem.

After

Have you ever seen a woman after it's over? After she's gone from single, to talking to, to dating, to boyfriend, to nothing? After what was supposed to be a walk in the park turned into a roller-coaster ride? After Hurricane Boyfriend came through and turned her entire house upside down, but every other house on the block went untouched? Have you ever tried to touch a woman who isn't healed? After the dust settles and she realizes she just wasted two weeks, two months, or two years on a man who didn't deserve even a phone call back? Have you ever been the man trying to get inside of a woman's heart, when *he's* still in her head?

Well, I have. And it was the hardest thing I have ever had to do in my entire life. And I don't think it's fair. But these are the types of problems that good men face when they become the firefighters for women's hearts, trying to put out a blaze that they didn't even start. Most men can't take the heat, so they get out of the kitchen. Then a guy like me walks up to her and calls her beautiful. And as much as she wants to tell me thank you, she doesn't. Because she's still hurting. And because she is still trying to put a scenario together in her head where it could have worked. It's rare that two people fall out of love at the same time; which means somebody is going to be left with all the questions, and with a contact in their phone that says "don't answer."

Love can leave you in some strange places when it doesn't take you home. What you have to understand is that love didn't take you there. He did.

So, after you're done crying, after you're done deleting all the text messages and the pictures, after you're done losing weight, changing your hair, and your phone number, I want you to sit down, take a deep breath, and say, "It's better to be a young fool than an old fool." Then go back to believing that there are men who only need one opportunity. Go back to believing that there are men who aren't afraid to love you accurately.

Believe that you are not too much woman. You're just caught in the drag, somewhere between "I miss my dad" and "where's my husband." Trust me, he is coming.

HEAL

I meet too many women who haven't recovered
From being in relationships with men
Who only appreciated them
When they were under the covers.
Or when they were all dressed up
Like trophies.
Playing it cool.
Laying with fools.
Whole time they were lonely.
I meet too many women
Chewed up.
Spit out.
Left on the side of the road.
Broken and cold.
Relationship roadkill.
Been in the streets so long
They forget how home feels.
How grown feels.
If you keep the key to your happiness
Around some man's neck,
A man who ignores all your
"I miss you" phone calls and "I'm bored" texts,
Only to reward him with more sex
Trying to screw you two back together?
Let it go.
If they aren't meeting your expectations,
Either bury your crown
Or let them know.
But you will no longer live in silence.
You will no longer resort to violence.
You will rise.

With a crown on your head
And a diamond between your thighs.
And any man who tries to tell you otherwise
No longer deserves the present that is your presence.

SELMA

I have a dream.
That every woman with half a man gets double the
courage.
That she puts as much effort as she spends on finding a
partner
Into finding her purpose.
That her list of partners will always be shorter than her
skirt is.
And when it's not,
She'll always know where the doctor,
Her block list,
Or a church is.
Because any evil that medicine or technology can't fix,
She'll give it to God.
And she'll never place her heart in the hands of a man
Who never asked for the job.
I have a dream
That every woman with half a man
Gets double the courage.
That she realizes that the one who carries her bags
Is just as cool as the one who buys her purses.
I won't stop
Until every woman knows she doesn't have to be perfect.
Until she knows that any man who wants her to be
will never love her.
So, don't bother.
Because the things we value the most we keep locked in
boxes.
Find the one who needs you to be his rock.
Not his diamond.
Someone who isn't afraid to put time in.

I have a dream.
That my work will birth a new breed of Phenomenal
Women.
Who find enough hours a day to work,
Go to school,
And still come home and raise phenomenal children.
And whether such a woman has the support of a man or
not,
She will never miss a meal.
And she will never mistake how love looks
For how it feels.

Sometimes you have to
look at yourself,
not as the woman you are,
but as the woman you will be.
Think about what she will want,
what she will deserve.
What she will be willing to
settle for.
Now, go chase that.
If a man decides to run with you,
let him.
But when he stops.
If he stops,
Remember
why you started running
in the first place.

Exchange

When I meet a woman who has a boyfriend, I always wonder, is she getting as good as she is giving? Is she being appreciated? Women have this habit of doing everything to the best of their ability. This includes loving. You might be wondering where the problem is. If she was in a relationship with herself, there wouldn't be one. But she's not. She's in one with a boyfriend.

And he doesn't try as hard as she does. And it makes me mad. A good woman is the cup that runs over to water the world. But who fills *her*? I meet so many women who are smart, who are strong, who are beautiful—who get around these men and then forget who they are. They forget where they come from. All isn't fair in love, all is earned. So if you're that girl, the one who bends over backward for her boyfriend, you just better be getting your back rubbed. Sometimes, I look into a woman's eyes when she says she has a boyfriend, and I don't see it. Call it, "Mike's intuition." So, for them:

There is a time and a place for everything. And boyfriend isn't the place to be suffering. Now, before you go overboard, I'm not talking about one of those arguments where you two call each other a bad name and don't speak for a week. That type of suffering is cute. He'll text you. They always do.

I'm talking about a different type of suffering, where you are low-key keeping somebody else alive; cooking, cleaning, encouraging, spoiling, kissing, hugging, praying for him, staying for him. You're doing it for no reason other than he's your boyfriend. And you still can't even get a good morning text.

The most expensive rose in the world is the Juliet Rose. When it debuted in 2006, the cost of producing it was estimated at $15.3 million. Trader Joe's has roses for $5. Gardens grow them for free. But the look on a woman's face, however, will always be priceless. Appreciation doesn't have a price tag. You just make sure you get enough consideration. Men have it too sweet for their girlfriends to be so sour. There are too many ways that attention can be shown for you to still feel unappreciated. I challenge you, not as a girlfriend, but as a woman, to only give what you get if the man isn't your husband yet.

Reciprocity

There's a word that not enough women
know the definition of.
Reciprocity:
"The practice of exchanging things with others
for mutual benefit."
Instead,
All they know is, "Be his rock."
"Be his better half."
Be his…"whatever."
Like you don't have needs.
Or a heart that bleeds.
Your existence
Is not the icing on some man's cake;
It is being the woman he baked it for.
Imagine.
If you weren't the only one giving it all they had.
If even though it was left on you
to put the bacon on the table,
He'd still be man enough to carry the bags.
Do you know what it feels like
To get a return on your investment?
When the product of all the work you put in
Is a man who doesn't leave you after you crown him?
If you don't, then you must be single.
Love might be patient, but it ain't lazy.
Your boyfriend is your evidence;
Proof that you're not easy. Proof you're not crazy.
Crazy for wanting more. Crazy for asking for more.
Crazy for reminding those who forget it.
Crazy for not stopping until you get it.
If you wanted to settle,

You could have stayed with your first.
And spent the rest of your life forgiving
and putting in work.
But you didn't.
So, make sure that when you call it "love,"
You're staring face to face
with a person who sees your fifty...
And raises you ten.
Love will always be a gamble.
Just make sure you're not the only one that's "all in."

The world will be at peace
When every man realizes
You can only take one woman
with you.
When every woman realizes
Any man that can't love you
Must miss you.
When relationships become
less like the tears
and
more like the tissues.

Feed

Too many women with boyfriends still go hungry: hungry for knowledge, hungry for affection, hungry for attention, hungry for respect. And for the life of me, I cannot understand how. I thought the beauty of being in a relationship in the first place was to have somebody to lean on when you can't handle life on your own. I thought that being in a relationship meant that you had someone who would invest in you—mentally, physically, emotionally—and in return, they would be the first in line to enjoy the fruits of their labor. These days, girlfriends produce a strange kind of fruit.

When a flower doesn't get water, it dies. When a flower doesn't get sunlight, it dies. When a flower is not planted in good soil, it is impossible for that flower to grow, to blossom, to produce anything of use. Some of these women are a different type of flower—the kind that grows through concrete. And while I respect their resilience, I pity their path. Since when did having a boyfriend make it okay for you not to grow? Since when did belonging to someone make it okay for you to starve? When did it make it okay for you not to be fed or encouraged, or not to be put in the best possible position to win? I'll tell you when—when you got a boyfriend and he got comfortable; or when you became a girlfriend and you got comfortable.

Most men forget that the same women they pull from, they must also invest in. Such a man forgets that being her boyfriend not only means he is lucky enough to be the first person to reap the benefits of a good woman, he is the first person she will look to for help. Somewhere, along the line, the help stops coming, but the women still allow themselves to be drained. The question is, who feeds the woman who feeds the world, if not her boyfriend? Too many women have their talents on reserve and restriction for men that have become so spoiled by the fruits they harvest that they forget to be the farmer. When this happens, I think you need to find a new place to grow.

RESERVATIONS

When I meet a woman who has a boyfriend
And I ask her if I can take her to dinner
And she refuses,
Only to come home to one of you losers
Who spent the majority of the afternoon on the couch,
But as soon as she opens the door,
The first thing you say out of your mouth is,
"What are we eating?"
I wonder,
Is her wishing she had taken me up on my offer considered
cheating?
Or is this the part where she's supposed to be strong?
Like she wasn't just at work all day long
For a boss who could never do her job,
But always tells her how.
After a drive that should only take fifteen minutes
Ends up being an hour,
When her feet hurt from walking,
When her teeth hurt from talking,
Is this the part where she's supposed to bite her tongue?
I'd rather you ask her could she be your dinner
Instead of making her make you some.
Too many women come home to a couch full of man
and a sink full of pans.
Thinking that somehow this is all part of the plan. It's not.
Call me. Call your mom. Call the cops.
Because you are being robbed.
What's a woman to do
When her boyfriend's house feels less like a second home,
And more like a second job
But run?

Or go to dinner.
And since you love him,
You'll remember
To order his favorite
And bring him back some.

Devil's Advocate

Now, of course, people are going to say, "Well, the only thing left for a boyfriend to do after he has become my boyfriend is to marry me, and maybe I'm not ready to get married yet. So, him 'just' being my boyfriend for now is okay." My response is, "If you are not ready for marriage, then you should be single." Now, here's where it gets tricky.

Sometimes, the reason why women get boyfriends is because they see a boyfriend as a Band-Aid for loneliness. They tell themselves, "I don't want to be single, but I don't want to be married." That's a totally different conversation than what we've been talking about.

Up to this point, we've been making it seem like "boyfriend" is just a thing that guys created to hold women hostage until the guys figured out what they wanted to do with the women or replaced them with somebody better. While that may hold some truth, some women are just as responsible for things being the way they are. Sometimes these women get together with boyfriends because they don't know what to do with themselves anymore. Sometimes, women get these boyfriends to use as a crutch because they're tired of walking through life alone. They're tired of coming home to an empty place. They're tired of going nights without being touched. So, they desire something. I would challenge them and say that what they desire is a husband.

In life, anything worthwhile that you get will be the product of hard work. Sometimes women see this road—going from being single to having a husband—and get confused about when and where to put the work in. All they know is that they're lonely. So, they tell themselves, "I have to put myself in a position to where I can fulfill these desires on a long-term basis." But rather than saying, "You know what? I'm going to take this job of finding my husband, or putting myself in a position where my husband can find me, more seriously," instead they say, "You know what? Maybe I should find a boyfriend." Do you see what you did there? You tried to cheat the process.

What you must realize is that when you cheat the process, you only cheat yourself. Not enough women see it, though. You know why? Because if you aren't wise enough to understand from the beginning that the whole idea of boyfriend is a fiction, you won't realize you're being cheated until the end. If he is truly the one for you, there should be no end. But the end comes when women take up with boyfriends who don't want to take them to marriage. They pull over to this rest stop called "boyfriend" and never leave. They never leave because technically, they don't have to. There isn't a judge, police officer, or lawyer who can make a man marry you. Ultimately, regardless of how much time, attention, money, and sex or how many children you give to a man, unless he wants to, he will never marry you. And if he doesn't, technically, the only person you can ever get mad at is yourself.

So to prevent you from suffering the same fate as the rest of the women who thought that by making sure they gave him everything he wanted now, in return, he'd give them that one thing they wanted later, we must make sure that this feeling of "wanting a boyfriend" isn't just misplaced emotions. If you're single and have "feelings" for someone, you have to make sure that these aren't voids that you can fill on your own. A lot of times these voids are the experience of women who just have too much time on their hands. I get it, though. There are only so many hours you can go work out, and there's only so many hours you can spend with your girlfriends. Sometimes your girlfriends supply more of the reasons you think you want a boyfriend than even you do. You start thinking to yourself, "You know what? Maybe I need a boyfriend," and then your girlfriends who have boyfriends reply, "Yes, maybe you do need a boyfriend, because I've got one, and look how that's working out for me." No. I challenge you not to do that.

I challenge you to not use boyfriend as that crutch—as a bridge between where you are and where you want to be. The only thing that can bridge that gap is time, not people. The road is meant to be long for a reason. Anyone can "act right" for ninety days. Imagine if there were no boyfriends, and he had to act right every day until the day he proposed. How many "boyfriends" would make it?

To be fair, I think a lot of the women wouldn't make it either. Sometimes, the women like that rest stop just as much as the boys do, and I'm going to tell you why. Sometimes boyfriend gives women the comfort of justifying some of the ridiculous stuff that y'all do for these men. Now, I bet you didn't want to hear that, but that's how I feel. I feel like sometimes women use this boyfriend thing to try to validate some of the stuff they do in advance of finding an actual husband. Sometimes women don't have the courage to say, "You know what? I slept with this man, and he has no attachment to me. You know what? I bore this man a child, and he has no attachment to me. I paid his rent. I paid his phone bill," et cetera. Having a boyfriend sometimes gives a woman the opportunity to rationalize some of the things she could not otherwise justify. So, as much as boyfriend kind of holds some women hostage, boyfriend is also a crutch for some women. You must remove the crutch.

Let's think about what we're asking for. I think for some women it's been a trial-and-error thing, and I think ultimately that for most people, the only way you're going to learn how to love is to sometimes learn how not to love in the process. Now, we can talk about love in relation to commitment if you want. But in short, I believe that you don't have to have commitment to have love. I've loved so many things and so many people to which I was never committed because I didn't love them for their commitment to me. I loved those things and people for what and who they were, independent of me.

You can love a flower while the flower is still in the dirt. You don't have to pick the flower up, take the flower home, put it in a pot, and make it your flower for you to love it. That's the beauty. That's raw love—when you can appreciate something where it is, untouched, in its natural state. Some of these flower-picking hands aren't even clean. So, I challenge you. Even if you're at this point where you feel like there's this void and you're almost certain that the void comes from lack of companionship...do not rush out and find a companion. Instead, begin to pack your bags, create your list, sort out your expectations, and set yourself out on a mission to find the man who will complete you.

I challenge you when you're at this point where you feel like there's this void and you're almost certain that the void comes from lack of companionship. The goal is not to rush out and find a companion. It's to begin to pack your bags, create your list, sort out your expectations, and set yourself out on a mission to find the man who will complete you.

Now, if along the way, you want to do some grown-up things, nobody's keeping track of what's going on in your bedroom but you and anybody you tell. There's no clicker. There's no doorman. There're no cameras, unless you allow them. So if the reason why you want a boyfriend is because between today and the day you find a husband, you feel like your body is going to need to be touched, then do that. But you don't need to use the concept of boyfriend as a justification.

CRAZY

Love will make you do some crazy things.
They won't seem crazy at the time.
But when you look back on it,
You'll realize that sometimes,
Love turns you into another person.
All real, no games.
All heart, no brains.
Just don't let it be all pain and no gain.
Sometimes love has you standing outside of his
apartment at 3 a.m.
And it could be because you went out,
Or because you just wanted to make sure nobody else got
in.
I guess sometimes "crazy" is your friend.
So, if you're the type of woman,
Who wears her heart on her sleeve,
Who would rather fight than leave,
Then get down on your knees
And pray.
That he'll see your "crazy" as a compliment and stay.
That all those titles, like "boo," "baby," and "bae"
Only happened because you were "crazy" about them,
And this type of "crazy" is the price that you pay.
If they can't handle your cup when it runs over,
If it makes them run,
Instead of telling you to come closer,
Then your relationship only has one soldier.
That means the only person you'll ever go to war with is
you.
When the mirrors and hearts break,
The only person on the floor is you.

Next time, do better.
Either see crazy, then be crazy.
Or find someone just as crazy as you,
Then make reservations for two.
Either way,
You won't be responsible for the repercussions
of what your crazy
Makes you do.

Compromise

By now, I hope you understand why I had to write this book. Somewhere along the way, someone came up with the bright idea that being in a relationship was the easiest way to fall in love, while forgetting that falling in love was never supposed to be easy. They said that being in a relationship was the fastest way to fall in love, while forgetting that haste most certainly makes waste.

I have proven to you that the very definition of "boyfriend" that you use does not have the same rules and expectations that you have for the word. Nowhere in any dictionary does the definition of boyfriend say exclusive. So why do you ask for it?

I have offered you an alternative. I have said that you can still commit to someone, but instead of that commitment being two people agreeing to be in a relationship, it's two single people who choose to only entertain one person.

I have given you statistics, warning you that mathematically it just doesn't make sense for you to devote this many of your prime years to one person without any guarantee. We have talked about God, your parents, and your girlfriends, and you've even gotten my personal stories about my experience with boyfriends.

If I haven't converted you into a person who no longer believes that being in a relationship with a boyfriend is the best possible course for a single person who one day aspires to be married, I hope that I've at least given you something to think about.

That being said, unless you are willing to step out on faith and say you know what, maybe Mike is right and we have been going through life doing this whole boyfriend thing wrong, then you are probably going to appreciate my book for it being a good read but will still give in to the pressure of a "good man" who isn't willing to put in the work past ninety days. You will give in due to the pressure of seeing your friends as well as strangers experiencing "relationships," and you will want one for yourself.

I am certain that at least one of you will have another boyfriend after you close this book, and I am already at peace with your decision. I'm at peace because like I said in the beginning, ultimately this is YOUR LIFE. Not mine. I am simply telling you that there's another path you can take.

So, for those of you who will still choose boyfriends, can I ask you one question?

What Are You Saving for Your Husband?

I pray every night that every woman either finds herself or a good man before she ever finds "the game." There are women in every corner of this planet, at this very moment, who are settling. They are being lied to, cheated on, disrespected, neglected, over-objectified, and under-protected.

And part of the reason why is because they are in relationships.

I can't stress enough how dumb this whole thing has become. I tried to find a better word, but I can't. There's no other word to describe a woman who gives a man the privilege of her mind, body, heart, and soul when he hasn't even taken on the responsibility—the mission—of being her husband. And if you try to tell me that boyfriends don't get those things, then you aren't even doing that right. Women only love one way: with everything they've got.

Then I think about the good men; the kind of man who always treats women with respect, and who never expects anything from a woman that isn't his. And then I think about when these two people finally meet—when such a man meets a woman who has been chewed up, spit out, and dragged through the mud by men who didn't even have to ask her to be their wife first. Then I consider what he will have to deal with in that relationship; the trust issues, the insecurities, the kids, the scars—everything left over when that "boyfriend" of hers took off. And I ask myself, is that fair to him?

This book will reach some people later in life, but it will reach everyone exactly when it needs to reach them. As long as there is air in your lungs and blood running through your veins, you still have time to get it right. This time, I want you to do me a favor. I want you to ask yourself what your most valuable asset is.

What is the one thing that makes you the woman some man is going to want to marry instead of the other woman? It's not my place to say if this talent is in your kitchen or your bedroom. All I'm asking for is one gift—one item to take off your menu, whether it be an appetizer or a dessert. Hold on to that for the man who will never think for a second that being a "boyfriend" is enough. The greater the gift, the harder the sacrifice. But if you do this, then on your wedding night, you will be able to say that you still have one thing that nobody else, up until today, has had the pleasure of experiencing. For that, he will love you ten times as much. If you can promise me this one thing, then you have my blessing to still have a boyfriend.

More poems...

MIRROR

When I see you,
I see everything a wise man would cherish.
Everything a weak one would be afraid of.
A collection of scars
That you're finally done hiding behind.
Finished apologizing for.
A raw beauty.
A "These are my flaws,
and you're going to have to accept them all" beauty.
A woman
Who might not be everyone's cup of tea,
But who had no intention of sharing herself with the world
anyway.
When I look in your eyes,
I see pain turned to purpose.
I see power.
But that doesn't always resonate with these cowards.
So, it's my duty to be the voice of your beauty.
I'm on a constant quest to change what your definition of a
man is
While being the photographer, security,
and president of your fan club.
You could go blind today and wouldn't miss a beat.
Foundation still flawless.
Eyebrows on fleek.
Any man who isn't his woman's number one fan
Is either lazy or crazy.
The shade comes too easy to not have your own personal
sun.
And there's nothing I'd rather do than shine for you.
Less excuses and more time for you.

What good am I, if I can't be your reflection?
Some days you won't feel as pretty.
Those are the same days I'll try harder.
Your insecurities are my to-do list.
The reward for you figuring out who you were
and staying that way.
So, the next time you look at the mirror,
And you don't like what you see,
Close your eyes, and remember me.

Groundhog Day

At 6 a.m., you're my alarm clock.
And with a face like that,
How could I wake up and not thank God for you?
At 7:20, you're the reason I get dressed in the living room,
Because watching you get ready for work is going to
make you late.
And make us parents.
At 8:15, we'll get dressed again.
At 11:45, there is a reminder in my phone that goes off.
It says, "You're lucky, don't mess this up."
At 11:46, I'll text you, "You're lucky, don't mess this up."
We'll laugh like it's a joke.
But we both know it's true.
The same world that broke our hearts finally sent us the
glue.
At 5 o'clock, you're the reason I don't stop at every sign
on the way home.
And if a cop decides to pull me over, I'll tell him,
"If you were going home to a woman as beautiful as mine,
You'd be in a rush too."
And no matter how expensive the ticket is,
It will never be as fine as you.
And you'll never have to worry about another woman,
Because every man knows when he gets his queen,
and mine is you.
When the money runs out, time will do.
At 5:45, you'll be home, and I'll be in traffic.
I'll text you asking if you need anything.
You'll reply, "Only you."
And I'll ask myself, what kind of man would let you go?
Only a fool.

But I've learned that one man's trash is another's treasure.

And one man's failure can be another's forever.

At 7, we'll eat dinner. At 9, each other.

And we'll always get over our arguments before we get

under our covers

And just before 10,

We'll get on our knees and ask God to forgive us for our

sins,

And then,

We'll fall into a deep sleep.

Just to wake up and do it

all over again.

ENOUGH

God made you for me.
And if the only thing that can keep us from being together
Is Hell or high water,
Then I will float on the hope that I'm already dead.
Because if waking up to you isn't heaven,
I don't know what is.
The problem with most men is they're too greedy.
They want to be able to have their cake and eat it too.
When the reason you even have a cake in the first place
Is to find a woman you love enough to feed it to.
And no matter how hungry I may be,
I promise, you'll always get the last slice.
You'll always need a minute to remember our last fight.
But when they ask you about the good times,
You'll giggle,
Put your ear on your shoulder, smile, and say last night.
You told me what your past was like,
But any man that's scared of a little baggage
Probably isn't strong enough in the first place.
I want to make you so happy on a regular basis
That you almost forget tomorrow's your birthday.
I want to be the father of your daughter.
Your supporter.
And when my love doesn't have your head in the clouds,
On the days you're not feeling beat from nude lips to
brows,
May the confidence I give you as your man
Make you feel like you can walk on water.
I just want to prove to you that you were always enough,
Just always attached to men
Who were never as good at giving it all as giving up.

And it hurt.
And it made you question your worth.
It made you wonder if you were worth putting in the work.
Know that the problem was never your heart,
Just the man whose hands it was in.

WHEN IT'S REAL

When it's real,
You'll feel it everywhere
From your ankles to your earlobes.
From the sex
To the feeling you get when they text.
And you won't be able to deny,
Only supply it.
Have you ever been in love before?
Where your sentences and your insecurities both get
finished,
Where five days out of the week,
You both want the same thing for dinner.
Have you ever felt like a winner?
Instead of like an employee
Who works first, then waits for the check.
Who gives her body up before she gets the respect.
Have you ever felt lucky?
How about equally yoked?
Have you woken up in the morning to tea and toast?
Have you been a witness?
To a man who loves you like you're a religion.
Who worships the ground you walk on.
Who always has a phone full of battery for you to talk on.
Do you know what it feels like not to be lied to?
When it's real,
You realize how fake everything else must have been.
You'll have the luxury of attaching a face
To the man of your dreams,
Plus,
You'll get to wake up to him.

TOGETHER

Fate brought us together.
Let's let love keep us there.
Love for ourselves.
Love for each other.
Love for love.
And together we will rule the world.
If not, let's run from it.
And whether we have enough to make it
to the other side of the earth,
Or the other side of a studio apartment,
Let's carve out our space in this crazy place
And live in it.
Unconditionally, and uninterrupted.
With enough memory in our phones to document the good
times,
And enough memory in our brains to carry us through the
bad.
I can't promise that we will always see eye to eye,
But I can promise that we will always be heart to heart.
We'll never spend more than we save,
Never work more than we play.
Never wish more than we pray.
And on the days when we aren't as perfect,
When your attitude and my pride
Have you in your feelings
And me on the couch,
Let's promise to never go to sleep angry or
argue over the internet.
Because when a relationship is in jeopardy,
The only thing worse than an audience
Are the actors.

And when they ask us why we choose each other,
In a world full of so many options,
We will tell them.
Life isn't about the ability to have everything,
It's the power of having only a few,
But that few being enough.
Let's make the doubters jealous and the believers hopeful
Together.

CROWN

Some days you don't know how you do it.
Half mother. Half magician.
Pulling tricks out of your bag
So your child won't have to know what it feels like
to miss meals
And a dad.
Because one is enough.
Being a single parent is tough,
Between diapers and daycare.
Most mornings you rise before the sun.
Most nights you just lie there.
Scared.
Wondering if this is the life God had planned for you.
Asking why he would send you your child before the man
for you.
Part of me feels bad for you.
But you can't survive off sympathy.
So, it's my responsibility to be the source of your energy.
Because in the process of being a parent, you made your
child's daddy an enemy.
Nevertheless,
You can't let the absence of dad leave mom stressed.
Because the fact still remains that you are blessed.
And as much as I want to be sad,
I can't.
All I can say is that it's time for you to put on your big girl
pants,
Because milk has become too expensive to cry over.
And sometimes you'll be left with more than some dirty
sheets
after you invite a guy over.

Sometimes one night can change everything.
And your focus will become more minivan and less
wedding ring.
In life.
Sometimes you have to play the cards you are dealt.
Sometimes that means being a parent by yourself.
And that's no more "right" than war or hunger.
But the truth is, no matter how you tell the story,
At the end of it you're still a mother.
Some women are more nervous than men in the beginning.
But it's hard to run when "inside of you"
Is where what you're running from is living.
So, you've got to stand and fight.
If not for you, than for this child that you gave a life.
And it won't be easy.
And it won't be cheap.
And you're going to lose a lot of friends.
And you're going to lose a lot of sleep.
And the rewards will be few.
The only one who knows the sacrifices will be you.
But whatever you do,
You can't quit.
Because some of the best moms the world has ever seen
Were birthed because dad wasn't shit.
So whenever your plate is full,
And your bank account is zero,
Read this poem,
And remember that you're my Hero.

EXTRA

Some nights you'll need more than a touch.
So it's my job as your man,
If ever your cup starts overflowing,
And those temperature sensors
under your T-shirt start showing,
Between these lips and hands,
I'll catch anything you might throw
at me.
And I promise I won't stop until we're both happy.
So tell me, where do you want me first?
No man ever wants to see his woman on all fours,
But if that's your favorite position,
I'll be the voice in your ear,
Pulling your hair, telling you, "It's all yours."
Sometimes you've got to go through pain to see pleasure.
So, I wonder if the reason you call God's name
whenever you're on top
Is because you see heaven.
I wonder what you taste like.
We don't even have to go all the way,
I'm cool with second base.
As long as I get a second to taste
why they call you "Woman."
Because the man in me realizes
that making sure you come first
will put me in first place.
You've got the cake, and I've got the candle,
it's only right that every day is your birthday.
The only good thing I've ever seen come from arguing
is the make-up sex.
So, I'd much rather make your day

before you even get out of bed.
Rolling over, the first thing you see
is my "good morning" text.
Only thing I want to fight about is who loves who more.
Furthermore, I promise that
the only time I'll make you cry
Is on our wedding day.
And I want our love to give people the same hope
That Obama did on Election Day.
I want that "we don't need to use condoms anymore" type
love.
That "the bedroom is too far,
so let's do it right here on the floor"
type love.
That "can you pick me up some pads
while you're at the store" type love.
The type of love that makes me want to buy the food,
cook it, and do the dishes,
As long as I can eat with you.
And the whole world could be at war,
I wouldn't care because when I came home and shut my
door
I would be at peace with you.
If my heart was a large pepperoni pizza,
I would want to give the last piece to you.
I wouldn't care if we shared a car and bank account
As long as I can count on you
to make me feel like I'm still special.
Promise to never take me for granted.
And smile just as hard five years from now
As you did the day after I met you.
Tell me you love me without speaking.
Then I'll know it's real.

WHEN HE LEFT

He took parts of her that she hasn't seen since.
And I haven't seen them either.
The woman she used to be,
Before she met the guy that was more boy than friend.
Before he put her in situation-ships where her only choice
was
either suck or swim.
Some women swallow more than their pride
For these guys.
Have you ever met a woman
Who treats her emotions like the closet you stuff
everything in
when you know you're about to have company?
Who treats her expectations like they're the junk
You jam under the bed
And not the portrait that's hanging over it?
They say you should never be jealous of an ex,
But I can't help it.
Because at least he's seen them.
All I'm left with are the scars.
Bullshit ex-boyfriends are used car salesmen
In towns with no lemon laws.
And her 'check engine' light just came on.
Good thing I'm a mechanic.
She has a heart that never makes it past the front door,
Inside of a body that can always make it to the bedroom.
The trust sucks. But the sex is amazing.
But it's probably because
It was the only thing they ever did together enough to get
perfect.
That and arguing.

But we don't even do that.
Have your ever tried to love a woman who only has
half a heartbeat?
One who hasn't cried yet.
Not because she doesn't want to,
But because she forgot how.
The same way burglary victims forget
When they don't have enough money to move,
Enough courage to buy a gun,
Because they're scared that one night they might use it
on themselves.
So, all they end up doing is buying more locks
And a Bible.
So that whatever wood and metal can't keep away,
God can try.
The same way she tries to pretend that she isn't different.
Have you ever met a woman who fell out of love with love?
That's like quitting school because of recess.
He left a taste in her mouth that no amount of wine
and homecooked meals could erase.
Like love was just her waiting two hours
in a ninety-four-degree amusement park line,
For a water ride that she didn't even get wet on.
Like a Christmas with none of the gifts you asked Santa for
on your list.
Like your idea of love is just a job that pays you less
than what you're worth,
But you're just supposed to walk in there
with a smile on your face every morning,
and be grateful that you have one.
The reason why more people aren't millionaires is
because they don't think they can be one.
Imagine being in love with a woman
who's waiting for the breakup.

Not on purpose,
But because she stops believing.
One who thinks her legs are only useful when they're open.
Who's always told she's beautiful before sex,
And never after work,
And doesn't go anywhere without makeup.
How do you love her? Answer: Slowly.
Because every man treated her like a commercial.
Love her like she's your favorite movie.
I can't love you unless you love you.

I'm in Your Corner

Boots laced.
Face covered in war paint.
Ready to ride for you.
Ready to put my pride, past, and promiscuousness aside for
you.
Ready to die for you.
And if it ever becomes too much,
If life's lemons ever make a mockery of your tear ducts,
I'll cry for you.
Because I can't hold water like you can,
I can't be half queen, half soldier like you can.
These other men couldn't see the beauty in your struggle.
That's why they couldn't love you.
But the silver lining in rejection is it brings you one step
closer to
your blessing.
So here I am.
Ready to take the leap.
So that on the lonely nights,
We'll sit on the phone at night, Counting the stars,
Counting the number of men who had this queen in their
deck,
But couldn't manage to play their cards.
And we'll laugh,
Because it will be over.
No more games, just peace.
You beauty.
Me beast.
And when the house can't hold us,
We'll take our love to the streets.
Dancing in the rain.

Dancing through the pain
Thankful for every battle that we lost.
Because if not,
These two paths would never have crossed.

IF

You closed your eyes,
She was the perfect woman.
Huge heart,
Massive mind,
Enormous energy.
Trapped between the woman she sees in the mirror
and the one you see in the magazine.
Only one of them is real.
But not enough men know how to handle a woman with
curves.
So they try to cut the fat from her waist with their words.
Like they don't hurt too.
Like her waistline is too big a problem for you two to work
through.
The criticism always hurts more than the crunches.
Coming from a man who always threatens to pack his bags,
But never her lunches.
I guess God gave her that gut so she could roll
with your punches.
Like her losing all this weight just to wait,
Hoping that one day you appreciate her for who she is,
Before she inherits that fifteen pounds after giving birth to
your kid.
These men can be cruel sometimes.
They'll make you the butt of their jokes
when they're not strong enough to sell you hope.
They're the fools sometimes.
This one's for the ones with a little extra to love.
A little extra to hug.
Who are held up by men who were supposed to be holding
them down,

Here is your crown.

And I don't care if you're a six or sixteen,

There is no shape or size requirement for a queen.

To the woman who starves herself for a man,

Hoping that a skinny her

will produce a more interested you:

Eat what you want.

And if anyone has a problem with it,

Devour them too.

RUNNING

With her Bible in one hand,
And her backbone in the other.
Looking for home.
Looking for grown
In a world full of boys
Searching for a pretty face
to play doctor with.
Broke.
A dime
Without two nickels to rub
together and line her pockets with.
Running,
Looking for a place to lay her head and her sorrows.
A place where she's welcome even after tomorrow.
Running
Away from boys who remind her of her father,
Who are only good at either coming and going
Or coming then going.
When the first man who was supposed to love you
Didn't stick around long enough to hear you say "daddy"
Running becomes hereditary.
Like water.
Searching for closure behind closed doors,
Only to find men more K-9
than King.
Who believe the only position a woman should ever be in
is on her back or on all fours.
With the audacity to use the same tongue that licks her
clean
to call her a whore.
Running

Looking for words that will stop the bleeding
Like, "I love you."
Looking for a man
Whose list of what he brings to the table
Is longer than the one of what he wants from you.
Praying.
'Cause it's hard to go to church on Sunday
When most Saturday nights
you're more sinner than saint.
When your body is tired of running
but the look in his eyes says
you can't.
Not this boy.
Not this night.
So, she runs.
Away from the demons,
But closer to hell.
So close to the edge.
That I don't know what to save first,
Her body or her soul.
Both were for sale.
And the only thing lower than her expectations was her
pride.
She couldn't remember the last time she made love or
cried.
Dying to have a conversation with a man that
doesn't involve the lips between her thighs.
Running
To a place where she can wake up
And not be asked why she hasn't left yet.
In the arms of a man who didn't care
if it's been two months
And they hadn't had sex yet.
But it is hard to dream about heaven

when hell is scratching at your thighs.
Trying to get inside.
When you've become so thirsty for a new life
that no tears fall when you cry.
Yesterday I met a woman.
Red hair, green eyes, brown skin.
Who stopped believing in rainbows.
She hasn't seen the sun since she was seven.
Is only called beautiful before sex or after eleven.
Whose luck has run bare,
Cup has overflowed
With disappointment
And despair.
And all I told her was I cared.
And we cried.
Because we knew
She didn't have to run anymore.

I'm Ready for Love

Two hearts
Two souls
One agenda.
An agreement of egos,
A compromise of futures.
The salvation of two sinners.
I'm ready to surrender
In a world full of war.
I'm ready to find home.
Ready to find my stability in your bones.
And one day a week we'll turn off our phones.
And love, uninterrupted.
No lies.
No pride.
Just two people
With one purpose.
Never let go.
I'm ready for permanent infatuation.
A crush
Deeper than Monday and Wednesday.
Thirstier than Thursday.
Freakier than a full moon on a Friday
On the thirteenth of the month.
Or a three-day weekend in the spring.
And the forecast calls for rain.
I just want to drown in you.
I just want to invite all of your exes to our wedding
So they can watch me put your crown on you.
Bigger, brighter.
And together
We will burn every bridge that ever betrayed us.

If you've got the fluid,
Here's the lighter.
They say the only way three people can keep a secret
is if two of them are dead.
But I'm never more alive than when I'm with you.
And I told God about you last night.
So, here's to our trinity.
I want to tattoo my name on the palms of your hands
So if ever you cry
Because I'm not by your side,
When you go to wipe your eyes
You'll remember me.
I'm ready for timeless.
'90s R & B,
'70s Soul,
Fifty years of marriage.
I know that it's out there.
It's just sometimes life gives you the lemons,
And it's up to you to find the sugar.
And I taste it too
Every time my lips press against the parts of you
That you can't post on Instagram.
I'm ready for peace
Peace with a promise
That no matter how hard life may get,
We will always get each other.
And we will always get over our arguments
Before we get under our covers.
Friends first,
Then lovers.
Partner in Crime,
Partner in Grind.
Then Wife,
Then Mother.

I'm ready for real.
Where I don't know who to be more afraid of,
My lovers or my friends.
I just want somebody willing to pick me up
Off the side of the road,
Broken and cold.
Open their car door
And their heart
And carry me to the end.
I don't care about you being rich
Or broke.
Because when we close our eyes,
We are all just some mixture of both.
All that I ask
Is when I can't see the forest for the trees,
You'll be a glimmer of Hope.
And when I'm hanging on by the last thread
At the end of my rope,
Too weak to revolt,
You'll be the love letter in my lunch box that says,
"I appreciate you."
Because the only thing better than loving
Is getting it back.
I'm ready for passion.
The kind where neither your burdens nor your bra
Ever make it to the mattress.
And I'll work a couple extra doubles
So you can work on getting your bachelor's.
And when the sun rises over our bedroom,
The first thing we grab in the morning
Won't be our phones, it'll be us.
And we'll make love again.
Because there's nothing like waking up
To a mouth full of your woman.

I just hope you can keep up.
And I'll love you
For who you are, first.
But for what you've done for me forever.
I swear to God.
All because you've resurrected parts of me
I thought were crucified.
Because you were the angel on my shoulder
That whispered "I love you,"
When the demon in the mirror said suicide.
You saved me.
Until I find that,
I'm better off being single.
Because it's hard to settle down
When settling was never part of the plan.
Raise your hand if you still believe in love.
If you still believe in miracles.
Now ball it up into a fist
And go fight.
Fight like your freedom depends on it.
Because if you don't,
You'll be just like the rest of them,
Ready for love.
But too afraid to do something about it.

WHEN MEN
GET MARRIED

It is the end of the road,
But the beginning of life.
It's the transition
From single to soul mate.
The promotion from all those years as "girlfriend"
To the reward of being wife.
Effective immediately.
And your only obligation is to love her repeatedly.
Because it's not about who comes,
it's about who never wants to leave.
It's witnessing him getting down on one knee.
It's watching your boyfriend
Turn into the man of your dreams.
When men get married,
It is the ball and chain that keep them grounded.
It's part "knowing where to look" and part
"Knowing when you've found out."
It's the insurance when you're "all in" and the dealer has an
ace.
It's the end of your training
And the beginning of your race.
It's looking the woman of your dreams in the face
And saying,
I don't want to wake up anymore.
I don't want to lie,
I don't want to see you cry.
I don't want to break up anymore.
Because only a fool would chase a dime
when he has a dollar in his pocket.

So, when men get married,
It's knowing what you've got while you've got it
And not wanting it to leave your side.
It's one of the few times it's cool to see a grown man cry.
Why?
Because she could have said no, but she didn't.
She could have told you to go,
but she didn't.
When men get married,
it is a promise to her,
her father and God.
Thanking them all for their help,
but taking over the job
Of loving her.
To put nothing above her.
Except her daughter.
And on the days her head isn't in the clouds,
When her face isn't beat from nude lips to brow,
May the confidence you give as her man
make her feel like she can walk on water.
When a man gets married,
It's to the woman he knows would leave today
If she ever thought that he thought 'boyfriend' was enough
to make
her stay.
So, go get your dress,
Your something old,
Your something new,
Your something borrowed
Your something blue,
Because in a few,
You'll be my wife.

The End.

Michael E. Reid

Michael E. Reid is a poet, author, speaker, and publisher from Philadelphia, Pennsylvania. Michael's story started after a failed relationship and unsuccessful suicide attempt, when he found himself in a hospital bed with a heavy heart and blank composition book. What started out as writing therapy for a man who lost his way exploded into one of the largest contemporary poetry inspired movements of our time.

Mike used his newfound talent as a writer to establish a social media platform dedicated to the inspiration, enlightenment, and encouragement of women. Five years removed from his first poem, Mike has penned four books, *Just Words*, *Just Words II*, *Dear Woman*, and *The Boyfriend Book* respectively. As of summer 2017, Michael's digital and print sales have ballooned to 250,000 copies sold. To date Mike has reached over 200,000 women across three social platforms "Just Mike The Poet."

Mike is always dedicated to giving his supporters what they want. He began doing one-off poetry performances in and around his hometown. Small spoken word cafes and restaurants would be jammed packed without proper event planning or marketing.

Mike, along with the help of "Vision" (Perry Divirgilio) and Jamarr Hall, set out to create their own poetry showcase. Resulting in three tours consisting of over twenty cities in three years—stretching from San Francisco to South Beach in Miami. For three tours over 50,000 people attended. In total, Mike has had over 160 independently organized events in thirty-three cities and five countries around the world. He also has spoken and performed at over twenty colleges and universities. Mike has sat on dozens of panels, facilitated workshops, delivered tear-jerking keynote speeches, and volunteered at a local female juvenile treatment facility.

Mike's publishing company, DOPE Publishing, specializes in teaching rather than taking from his clients. Since its inception in 2014, Mike has assisted in the publishing of more than forty books for other authors. Combined, his authors have sold an additional 100,000 books in their own right. It is apparent that Mike has dedicated the life he almost lost to other people.

D.O.P.E. PUBLISHING

CONSULTING | CREATING | PRINTING
PROMOTION | PUBLISHING

D.O.P.E. (Dreams On Paper Entertainment) specializes in EVERY aspect of publishing. What separates D.O.P.E. from other DIY companies is its comprehensive and all-inclusive list of services, with clients learning the ins and outs of the publishing process. Furthermore, in most cases, D.O.P.E.'s clients will keep 100% of their royalties.

Here at D.O.P.E., our goal is to assist you throughout the entire process of successful self-publishing, while minimizing cost and maximizing your potential for success.

START YOUR JOURNEY
DOPEPUBLISHING.COM